## "You'd make an ideal mistress."

Luke's grip tightened as Paula tried to free herself. "If I could stomach your deceitfulness," he finished angrily.

"I don't intend being deceitful anymore," Paula said hollowly.

For a second, something flashed in the depths of his eyes, and Paula felt a stir of hope that he cared for her. But it was obvious that he had no intention of continuing their relationship.

"You don't expect me to believe that?"

"I only wish things had been different."

"So do I."

Suddenly she was crushed against his chest, and a potent surge of longing swept over her as his mouth descended to hers. It might be the last time Luke would kiss her, so why deny herself?

# Books by Margaret Pargeter

These books may be available at your local bookseller.

Don't miss any of our special offers. Write to us at the following address for information on our newest releases.

Harlequin Reader Service
P.O. Box 52040, Phoenix, AZ 85072-2040
Canadian address: P.O. Box 2800, Postal Station A,
5170 Yonge St., Willowdale, Ont. M2N 6J3

# MARGARET PARGETER

## model of deception

**Harlequin Books**

TORONTO • NEW YORK • LONDON
AMSTERDAM • PARIS • SYDNEY • HAMBURG
STOCKHOLM • ATHENS • TOKYO • MILAN

Harlequin Presents first edition February 1986
ISBN 0-373-10861-3

Original hardcover edition published in 1985
by Mills & Boon Limited

# CHAPTER ONE

SOMETIMES Paula couldn't believe what had happened to her life. In a short space of time it had altered completely. One week she had adoring parents, eager to grant her every wish, and a fiancé constantly declaring his love for her. The next week both her parents had been killed in a motorway accident and her supposedly devoted fiancé had departed with the speed of a rocket when her father's questionable business activities had come to light.

From being a cherished only child—spoiled rotten, she had overheard one charitable person say—she was now alone in a world which she was fast discovering had little time or sympathy for a girl without a penny to her name. The people who had once fawned over her now patronised her, if they bothered to notice her at all. Invitations stopped with the precision of a guillotine, especially when it became known that Lord Doobray's son and heir had also cast her off.

Because neither financial ruin nor a broken engagement succeeded in marring her fabulous beauty, men still pursued her, but instead of treating her with their former respect, they now expected her to jump into bed with them at the drop of a hat. The evening before, at a second-rate party, when a scruffy type she had just been introduced to began pawing her intimately, she had slapped his face.

'You're all the same!' she had spat, rushing home in a taxi she couldn't afford, tears of anger and self-pity running down her cheeks. Letting herself into her flat, she had tossed back her mane of red-gold curls and made a silent vow. One day some man was going to pay for what Ian Doobray had done to her, but, supposing she had to wait years, it would be someone with far more to lose than scum like Len Walker, the man whose face she had just slapped.

The opportunity, however, came sooner than she expected and from an unexpected source. It arrived in the form of a letter from the property company from whom she mortgaged her flat. They wrote, they said, for the third time, asking her to contact them regarding overdue repayments. When she did, reluctantly, she was given an appointment to see them the following morning.

Damn! she thought, slamming down the receiver, hoping it damaged someone's ears. She hated getting up that early when she wasn't modelling. Giving vent to increasing frustration, she flung the paperback she was reading across the lounge. She hated modelling, too. It had been fun when she had merely done it to pass the time, but not since she had been forced to do it in order to earn a living. Not that she ever did more than was absolutely necessary. Lately she had refused a lot of jobs without realising how short she was getting of money. Making a hurried phone call to her long-suffering agent, she accepted the swimwear assignment in the Caribbean. She could always tell Cranfords she had this coming in, which should keep them out of her hair for at least a few weeks!

With a lazy sense of self-indulgence, Paula slid slowly out of bed the next morning. Yawning her way delicately to the adjoining bathroom, she filled the pink marble bath full of hot water. Squeezing in half a bottle of Balmain bath foam, without a thought as to where the next lot was coming from, she let over a hundred pounds' worth of sheer satin nightdress fall carelessly to the floor. Immersing herself gracefully in the scented depth of the tub, she refused to believe that this luxury, which she had known from childhood, would not be hers for ever.

Afterwards, dried and perfumed with her favourite eau fraiche from Nina Ricci Fleur de Fleurs, she dressed with more care than usual in a soft, elegant two-piece from Chanel. Realising she might need all the charm she possessed if she hoped to weather this particular crisis without losing her flat, she tried to ensure that her appearance would help her effectively. Viewing herself when she finished, she was sure it would. Her red-gold curls gleamed in cultivated disorder while her cool green eyes shone from a face of remarkable beauty. Her skin was unblemished and creamy, a perfect setting for a mouth that curved softly, like the luscious pink petals of a rose. Above this was a slightly tip tilted nose and the most entrancing dark golden lashes and brows.

In contrast to the searching inspection she gave her face, the glance she bestowed on the rest of herself was so brief she might never have bothered. At twenty-two, she had the kind of figure that attracted wolf-whistles in the street, but it had never interested her greatly. Ian used to say that her figure was the most provocative and disappointing thing about her—the latter because she had refused to let him make love to her before they were married. She had never told him that she hadn't slept with him because she hadn't been tempted to, or that she had never wanted to sleep with another man. But although she had kept it from him that she was frigid, she had intended making him a good wife. It was he, in the end, who had let her down, not the other way around. She had counted on becoming Lady Doobray one day and she would never forgive him for depriving her of the distinction of that!

When the chime of a clock reminded her that if she didn't hurry she was going to be late for her appointment, Paula turned from the mirror to begin her journey through the busy London streets. After the first hundred yards she signalled a cruising taxi, telling herself idly that she would begin economising after this. Moodily she thought of her father's luxurious limousines, all of which had been sold after the crash. The flat was all she had left, and though it was mortgaged up to the hilt, she was determined to hang on to it.

Arriving at her destination, she was shown into a large office where she found two middle-aged men waiting for her. She looked at them in surprise, remembering how, the last time she had been here, when she had arranged for her father's mortgage to be transferred to her own name, she had only seen one of the clerks. These men looked far too important to be mere clerks, yet she was even more surprised when they introduced themselves as Neil and Denis Cranford, the brothers who owned the firm. Surely this wasn't normal procedure?

'I—er—understand I'm a few weeks in arrears...' she began uneasily, after they had invited her to sit down.

As the brothers reseated themselves, Denis Cranford cleared his throat delicately. 'The matter of your mortgage repayments wasn't the sole reason why you were asked to come here this morning, Miss Edison, though the fact that you owe us a rather substantial sum of money does have some bearing on the matter we would like to discuss. If you would allow us, my brother and I have a proposition we would like to make.'

'A—proposition?' Paula stared at the two men suspiciously while scrambling to her feet.

'It's a business proposition, Miss Edison,' Neil Cranford said quickly, a flicker of dry comprehension in his eyes. 'Please don't be alarmed.'

Paula relaxed in her seat again, forced to remember she was in no position to walk out with her nose in the air. And, despite herself, she felt curious. And the Cranfords intrigued her. Their benign appearance, she suspected, was totally misleading. Behind it, she would be willing to bet, lay two hard-headed business men, and it might pay her to at least listen to what they had to say.

Neil Cranford glanced at his brother, then continued, 'We knew your father, Miss Edison, and can understand the rather straitened circumstances you now find yourself in. Considering everything, we wondered if you would be interested in working for us.'

Paula didn't think it odd that they had known her father. She decided to overlook the remark about her present circumstances, but she couldn't see how she could be much use to them. Fearing she might be wasting their time as well as her own, she said quickly, 'I'm afraid I know nothing of your kind of business, Mr Cranford. I model as it's about all I can do, not because I'm fond of it. Although,' she added hastily, for fear they wondered where the money she owed them was coming from, 'I get plenty offers of work. I have an assignment in Barbados next week.'

'Barbados!' Neil exclaimed, while Denis threw up his hands and laughed, 'Amazing!'

Confused, Paula glanced from one to the other, then her normal intelligence began working again. 'Is it some kind of promotional work you have in mind?'

'Not exactly,' Denis sobered. 'What we have in mind is something rather different from what you're doing now, Miss Edison, but it should be well within your range. We have a problem which we haven't been able to solve, and we believe you might be able to help us.'

'If you tell me what it is—and if I can,' Paula conceded cautiously.

'It's entirely up to you, of course,' Denis watched her face as he slowly fed her curiosity. 'If you did agree to help us you would be well rewarded. We would be prepared to write off the balance still owing on your mortgage, in addition to a sum of money,' he named a figure that made Paula blink. 'All this,' he concluded smoothly, 'should you agree to do what we ask. And succeed.'

'And if I don't succeed?' Paula tried to seem detached as she put the question. She wondered what kind of job could be worth paying that much to anyone.

Denis smiled quite kindly. 'If you don't, providing we're convinced you've tried, then the flat will be yours free for a year and we'll pay your expenses home.'

Paula drew a sharp breath. She wasn't foolish enough to imagine that such largesse was being offered for nothing. Such a reward might have to be paid for very very dearly! 'Home from where?' she asked slowly, playing for time.

'From Barbados,' Denis replied. 'That's why we were so delighted when you mentioned that you were going there. It couldn't be more convenient. When you finish your modelling job you could simply carry on, working for us.' He gazed steadily into her widening eyes and after a short silence, asked gently, 'Well, would you like to hear more, or have you changed your mind?'

Because she found it difficult to decide, another moment elapsed before she said slowly, 'You tempt me.'

'I'd like to do more than that,' he smiled. 'But, as I've just said, it's entirely up to you.'

When he didn't push her in any way, Paula nodded. There seemed no harm in hearing what they had to say. She wasn't committing herself in any way.

As Neil Cranford rose to fetch them each a drink from the bar in the corner, Denis began talking briskly. In seconds his manner revealed him as the astute business man Paula had suspected him to be.

'For the past three years,' he said, 'my brother and I have been trying to buy a certain island in the Caribbean. We're an international firm and would like to develop this island for commercial purposes, but its owner refuses to sell. Last year he agreed, then he backed down at the last minute. We've tried everything we can think of to make him change his mind. Everything, that is, except a beautiful woman.'

Whatever Paula had expected to hear, it wasn't this. Incredulously she broke in. 'You can't be seriously suggesting that I could persuade this man to sell you his island, just because I happen to be a model? I have no idea what he's like, but he must be wise enough to be familiar with this kind of approach? Anyway, beautiful women, over there, are two a penny.'

Denis took a gulp of his tea, waiting impatiently

until she calmed down. 'If you'd kindly let me finish,' he said dryly, 'you may have grasped the general idea, but you're quite wrong in thinking we're considering sending you there as a kind of glorified salesgirl. You must give us credit for more subtlety than that. We haven't discussed any definite tactics—we're leaving that to you, but we do have a general plan within which we would like you to work. Initially we were going to ask you to go to Barbados as an ordinary tourist and probably get to know Mr Armstrong by taking a boat out to his island. Plenty of people trespass on these private islands, whether by accident or design. They may be warned off, but it's rarely considered a crime. It shouldn't be difficult for a girl like you to meet Mr Armstrong and get yourself invited to stay. And once there, it should be relatively easy to make him fall in love with you, and, after that, to persuade him to go and live elsewhere.'

Paula felt stunned as well as outraged when Denis stopped speaking. Did they think she was crazy? She had never heard of anything so utterly absurd in her life! Sweeping back her red-gold curls with an angry gesture, she exclaimed indignantly, 'Just what kind of a girl do you think I am?'

The two brothers shrugged simultaneously. Denis didn't try to hide the fact that he'd done his homework properly. 'You've been engaged and known plenty of men. Since you ask, I should imagine you're a girl with considerable experience. You don't think we'd employ a naïve little innocent for such a job, do you?'

Attempting to control her rising fury, Paula drew a deep breath. They certainly didn't believe in sparing her feelings! They must have had her investigated thoroughly, even if their conclusions were slightly off the mark. In a way she could admire their originality, but weren't they taking too much for granted?

'I may have been around,' she allowed coldly, fixing them a baleful glance, 'but I don't happen to believe in love. If this Mr Armstrong shares my sentiments, or rather, the lack of them, then your brilliant plan wouldn't stand a chance.'

'It's a gamble we're willing to take,' Denis replied confidently. 'This time I don't think we would fail.'

Such optimism was beyond Paula. 'Well, just suppose this man did fall for me,' she argued, 'there's no guarantee that I'd be able to entice him away from his island. If he did fall for me, wouldn't it make him more inclined to stay?'

'Not if you made full use of your brains and beauty,' Denis said meaningly, his eyes flicking over her. 'Luke Armstrong is only in his thirties, with, from what I've heard, more than his share of libido. Handle him properly and you should have no trouble.'

Paula knew better than to take that as a compliment. Her green eyes sparkled angrily as she persisted sarcastically. 'If I did manage to persuade him that a Caribbean island wasn't for me, I can't believe he'd be willing to go elsewhere unless I promised to have an affair with him. You surely wouldn't expect me to go as far as that?'

Apparently they did. 'An affair,' Denis shrugged, 'can be over in a week. Even marriage, today, need scarcely last longer. We're offering you a great deal of money, Miss Edison.'

She began to feel she would be earning it. Not that for a moment, she assured herself hastily, she had any intention of doing what they asked, now that she knew what was involved, but it was interesting to learn what lengths some people would go to in order to get their own way.

She heard Denis continuing suavely, 'We're a property company, Miss Edison. We acquire land all over the world. An island like the one we're talking about can be worth a small fortune if properly developed. We don't prosecute people, Miss Edison, in order to succeed, and we aren't leeches, but we are convinced that Luke Armstrong would sell if he had the right incentive. It's not as if he depends on the island for a livelihood—wherever he gets his money from, it's not there.'

'I'm sorry!' Suddenly coming to her senses, Paula jumped to her feet, trying to hide her revulsion. 'I really can't do as you ask,' she protested. 'You'll have to find someone else.'

No surprise was evinced at her reactions—or dismay. That no obvious sign of the latter was displayed by either of the brothers failed to put her on her guard. 'Why not think it over and let us know?' Denis suggested smoothly, beside her in a flash. 'On reflection, you might find it's too good an offer to turn down, and if you did take it up we'd like you to know there won't be any threats or pressure. You'd be paid on results, and I've already stated our terms if you don't succeed.'

'I'm sorry!' Paula repeated firmly, already on her way to the door. Then despairingly she remembered something she had almost forgotten. 'If I don't agree,' she said slowly, 'what about the money I owe?'

Denis waved a hand carelessly as he opened the door for her. 'Oh,' he smiled, 'I'm sure we'll be able to arrange something. But have you ever thought,' he added craftily, 'should you accept our offer, you might never be troubled with mortgage payments again?'

The following week found Paula relaxing against the bulkhead of a small cabin cruiser which was hopefully searching the sparkling waters of the Caribbean for a deserted island. Paula had come to Barbados with two other models and Ron Davis, their cameraman, on a commission from a famous fashion house. So far they had only worked on the main island, but now Ron was looking for a slightly different kind of background.

Because he hadn't found any place he considered suitable during the whole of the previous day, this hadn't improved his disposition, which was never very agreeable, anyway. Paula hated working with him and she didn't think the plan for her to quarrel with him before they went home would be very difficult to carry out.

The other two girls had stretched lazily on deck to resume the sleep which such an early morning start had interrupted. Ron lounged silently at the tiller, drinking coffee while moodily contemplating the empty distances. There was no one to disturb Paula's uneasy thoughts. Ian Doobray had jilted her, but she was beginning to wonder if she had been wise in allowing his defection to influence her to the extent of not caring what she did. Last week, after her first meeting with the Cranfords, she had had no intention of doing as they asked. That she had signed a contract with them the next day still amazed her, though the reasons behind her change of mind remained as clear as ever. After a worrying night, the chance of getting rid of her mortgage had proved irresistible. The money that went with it had also proved too great a temptation to resist, especially when she had realised it was enough to keep her in comfort for the rest of the year.

After taking time to think about it carefully, she had decided she would be crazy not to accept the offer the Cranfords had made. Why should she let someone like Luke Armstrong stand in her way? From all accounts, he was a man who could look after himself, and if she did have to promise to sleep with him in order to persuade him to leave his island, if she kept her wits about her she might easily escape before things went as far as that. Even if he caught her up and forced her to keep her promise, she doubted if he would want to sleep with her twice. As she was totally inexperienced, she didn't think it likely that he would appreciate her inability to respond to him any more than Ian had done. The likelihood of Luke Armstrong falling for her seemed remote, but, if anything like that did happen, she would take great pleasure in throwing whatever feelings he developed for her back in his face, once the business of the island was settled. It would be just retribution for what Ian had done to her and would give her enormous satisfaction.

While the whole affair sometimes seemed incredibly

far-fetched, she was getting used to it. That she had nothing worked out yet didn't seem to matter. All the main details were being taken care of by the Cranfords, so she had nothing to worry about. She had merely to find Luke Armstrong and his island and let things take their natural course. She was hoping that Ron might come across the island by accident, so she might have a chance to weigh Mr Armstrong up before the others returned to London and she was left in the Caribbean alone with him, but she wasn't counting on it. Lazily, Paula stretched, turning her face to the rising sun. Only rarely were problems as easily solved—it was too much to expect.

She wasn't paying much attention to what Ron was doing, but when he suddenly shouted, 'Land ahoy!' with all the triumph of a shipwrecked sailor, she jumped to her feet and looked around.

'There it is!' he pointed, rather unnecessarily, Paula thought, as they were almost upon it, to a fair-sized island surrounded by sandy beaches, shaded by majestic palms. 'Could just be the place I'm looking for,' he laughed, clearly in a better mood.

Paula wandered to the low rail where Lena and Coral joined her. Lena said wearily, 'I was hoping he wouldn't find anything. I could have slept all day.'

'Me too,' yawned Coral.

Paula laughed, though not unkindly. 'Why don't you try an early night for a change?'

Coral retorted dryly, 'You only went to bed early because you weren't enjoying the party and you couldn't think of anything else to do.'

Paula shrugged. They were staying at a top-class hotel where the entertainment was good, but somehow, last night, it had bored her. Gazing at the fast approaching island, she was suddenly glad she had had a good night's rest. If this did happen to be where Luke Armstrong lived, she might need all her wits about her. She might only have a short time in which to attract his attention and make him interested in seeing her again.

Now that the chance of meeting him no longer seemed so improbable, she was struck by further feelings of uncertainty. For the first time she found herself wondering about Luke Armstrong as a man, rather than just some faceless figure whom she had agreed to try and deceive. What if she found him repulsive? He could even be dangerous, though the Cranfords had promised he was none of these things. If she was to meet him now, it would certainly help her to decide what he was like for herself, but because the remuneration she was to receive for this job was important to her, she felt she would as soon wait until the others had left before meeting him, when she would have less chance to change her mind.

Ron tied the boat to the small jetty he had spotted in one of the coves. He had done enough sailing to enable him to do this with ease. Paula watched him dispassionately. He could do a lot of things well but was inclined to be vindictive and bad-tempered when he came up against problems. She would hate to think that Luke Armstrong was anything like him, but she supposed if he was she would just have to make the best of it.

'Let's hope we have the place to ourselves,' Ron muttered, as they went ashore.

The island looked deserted. Ron didn't attempt to explore, but confined himself to a quick tour of a couple of beaches while the girls waited for him to make up his mind. Eventually he chose a spot he considered suitable and, after setting up his equipment, asked Paula to pose first, in the costume she was already wearing. This took quite a time, then he sent her back to the boat to change while he took shots of Lena and Carol.

It was half an hour before she returned, as Mrs Hartley, who was in charge of the party, had fussed a lot over her make-up, but as Ron still wasn't finished with the other girls, she sat down in the shade of a tree. The silence of the early morning was uncanny. Paula shivered as she gazed out to sea. The island was beautiful but lonely. There would be too much time here to think. She preferred places like London where there was plenty going on. This island was wonderfully soothing, but too quiet.

It was then, as her eyes wandered, that she noticed a man striding towards them along the shore. She didn't think he had noticed her as his attention seemed fixed on the boat by the jetty. Then, as he obviously caught sight of Ron, his footsteps swerved swiftly in his direction.

Because she wasn't so far away, Paula saw the expression of annoyance that flashed over Ron's face as the man approached, but she was too busy staring herself to feel any sympathy for him over such an untimely interruption. The stranger must have been swimming, because his hair and shoulders gleamed wetly, as though he had just come out of the sea. Only the brief shorts he wore were dry, which made her suddenly realise he had been swimming with nothing on. But what disturbed her more was his general appearance. He was well over six foot and substantially built. His broad shoulders and taut thighs were powerful, as were his muscular arms and long legs. She couldn't see his face, as he was now standing with his back to her, but she drew a sharp breath at the arrogant set of his dark head. Even from this distance, the angle of it looked menacing. Apprehensively, Paula shivered. This couldn't possibly be the man the Cranford brothers had described! According to them, Luke Armstrong was the mildest of men. If this was Luke Armstrong, they must have been crazy in believing a girl like herself capable of dealing with a man like him!

Rather than sit trembling, she rose silently and crept closer. She was just in time to hear the stranger saying to Ron, 'You do realise you're trespassing, don't you? This is private property.'

Ron didn't try to hide his irritation and his voice was belligerent. 'Your—property?'

'Yes.'

The clipped edge to the stranger's voice must have warned Ron to tread carefully. After a moment's hesitation, he apologised politely, 'I'm sorry, I had no idea.'

The man acknowledged his apology with the merest inclination of his head. 'I'd appreciate it if you would leave immediately.'

'Couldn't I take just a few more shots?' pleaded Ron. 'We're on an assignment and I'm almost finished.'

The man's head turned to where Lena and Coral sat like two beautiful mermaids on some rocks, obviously without a flicker of interest. 'I'm afraid not.'

Recognising that Ron was on the verge of losing his patience, Paula moved forward instinctively. Hearing her behind him, the stranger swung around swiftly, his air of cold indifference fading as his glance fell on the advancing girl. His dark brows lifted slightly and they were both suddenly staring at each other tensely. Paula somehow couldn't look away. 'Hello!' he drawled softly, his eyes narrowing. 'Where did you spring from?'

Quick to latch on to anything that might be used to his own advantage, Ron told him hastily that she was Paula Edison, one of his team of famous London models. Then he introduced Lena and Coral and himself, as their cameraman.

The stranger nodded to the others but shook Paula's hand. 'My name's Armstrong,' he replied, almost absently, 'Luke Armstrong.'

Paula felt a peculiar sense of shock. With the greatest difficulty she remained calm while her head whirled. Luke Armstrong's expression seemed to soften and darken as he revised his earlier decision and told Ron he could carry on, without once taking his eyes off her.

'I never expected to find someone like you on the beach, this morning,' he smiled, as Ron walked away.

Paula was glad she was wearing a matching cover-up over her bikini as he made a steady inspection of her tall slender figure. He had silvery grey eyes which were affecting her oddly. 'We didn't expect to see anyone, either,' she managed to retort lightly. 'We thought the island was deserted.'

'I live here,' he kept hold of her hand though she tried to free it, 'but apart from myself and a couple of servants there's no one else.'

Paula gulped, convinced that this must be the man whom the Cranfords had sent her to find. Everything about him added up. His name, for a start, and his age; he looked about thirty-four. He even appeared to have more than his fair share of sex appeal, which the Cranfords had mentioned too. Paula glanced at the covering of dark, curly hair on his chest and a tremor ran through her.

Despite this, she quickly recovered her equilibrium and became coolly sensible again. She wondered what he would say if she were to reveal that she knew all about him. Then, reminding herself that she should be making the most of her undoubted good fortune in meeting him like this, instead of wasting time speculating, she smiled at him and commented wistfully, 'Living on an island must be wonderful. I quite envy you.'

'You can't be serious?' he teased. 'A beautiful girl like you must be more attracted to big cities.'

'Not always,' she denied, glancing at him demurely from under long lashes. 'I'll admit the city might win if it came to choosing a permanent place to live, but I could happily settle here for a week or two.'

'Consider yourself invited,' he smiled, 'for as long as you like.'

Paula didn't know whether she was vexed or relieved when Ron called that he was ready for her. 'This shouldn't take long, Mr Armstrong,' he added, clearly regretful about taking her away.

Paula said suddenly, as Luke released her cramped fingers, 'We mustn't detain you. Watching this kind of thing can get pretty boring, and you must have better things to do.'

'I can't think of any,' Luke replied coolly, then, turning to Ron, 'I'd like you all to come and have breakfast with me when you're finished.'

'Great!' Ron accepted, looking pleased. 'We should be through in an hour.'

As the camera clicked and she followed Ron's intermittent instructions, Paula was aware of Luke's eyes on her all the time. Some of her costumes were so brief she felt an unfamiliar heat in her cheeks, but he didn't seem to notice. He appeared to enjoy watching Ron making her pose in more different positions than she thought necessary. Only once, when Ron shouted at her, did his face harden. That he didn't like Ron shouting at her might be no bad thing, Paula reflected, remembering how she was supposed to fall out with Ron at the end of the trip.

After the morning session was over they collected Mrs Hartley and set off along a well trodden path to Luke's house. The three girls changed into shorts and sun-tops, which was all they had with them. Paula ran a hand over the tense muscles at the back of her neck. Posing in front of a camera for hours always tired her. She thought with relief how good it would be to give it up for a while, which she might be able to do if she managed to part Luke Armstrong from his island.

He led the way, walking beside her in front of the others, holding her arm. She wasn't sure what to make of him, his eyes were too enigmatical, but she told herself she only needed time to get him summed up. She disliked the way he persisted in hanging on to her and, more than once, glanced at the proprietorial hand on her arm, a glance which, if he saw it, he chose to ignore. He seemed quite content to amble along by her side, adapting his longer strides to her shorter ones, a look of satisfaction on his bronzed face that put her uneasily in mind of a purring tiger.

His house came as a surprise. Somehow, from the Cranfords, she had gained the impression that he lived in a gracious mansion. The building they approached was large enough, but utilitarian-looking rather than beautiful. There were no green lawns surrounding it either. The gardens looked slightly overgrown and there was no sign of what Paula considered the basic necessities, such as a tennis court and a swimming pool.

'What do you think of my home?' Luke Armstrong muttered in her ear as they went inside.

She glanced curiously at the bare floors and hard cane furniture. There was plenty of space but little comfort. 'It needs a woman's touch,' she said frankly, 'but you probably like it as it is.'

'I do,' he smiled, and she sensed that her outspoken reply hadn't surprised him. For all he was fond of his house, he must be aware of its lack of modern amenities.

'I like it!' Coral must have overheard their conversation and glanced past Paula with a dazzling smile for Luke Armstrong as she stretched her sinuous body into one of his cane chairs. 'It's nice and cool here. I get so fed up with hotels.'

Paula, recognising Coral's little game, felt a sense of relief when Luke didn't issue her the same invitation to stay as he had given her. He did, though, ask them all to spend the day with him. 'It will make a change,' he said smoothly. 'You can feel free to do as you like.'

Everyone but Ron accepted happily. Ron didn't seem to relish the prospect. 'I suppose we can stay a few hours,' he agreed reluctantly, 'but we must get back to Barbados this afternoon. There's still plenty to do—and we're supposed to be working.'

The morning passed pleasantly enough, in spite of Ron's dour observations. Luke's servants provided a delicious breakfast and waited on them hand and foot. There might be a lack of normal comfort, Paula reflected, but the food and service couldn't be complained about. The presence of the servants gave her an encouraging feeling of security. If she did return here, she wouldn't be alone with Luke. The middle-aged housekeeper and her husband would make excellent chaperons.

After they finished eating, Luke offered to show them over the island, but this time only Paula accepted. The others just wanted to lie in the sun and perhaps swim. Coral looked at Luke wistfully, but she hated walking.

Paula wasn't that fond of it herself, but she was keen to discover all she could about Luke Armstrong. She didn't think he would be more than she could handle, but spending some time with him might help her to decide. There was still time to tell the Cranfords she had changed her mind about the job they wanted her to do for them. Patting a red-gold curl in place, she slipped her Polaroid glasses on to her elegant little nose and followed Luke confidently.

# CHAPTER TWO

L̲ᴜᴋᴇ A̲ʀᴍꜱᴛʀᴏɴɢ's house sprawled on a wide plateau high above the beach and there were wonderful views of the island and crystal-clear seas. The mountainous backbone of the island was clothed in green vegetation and the valleys were full of lush tropical flowers. For a while, as they wandered through one of the valleys, Paula was enthralled by the variety of shrubs and trees, but as the undergrowth gradually became too dense to penetrate easily, Luke suggested they went down to the shore.

'Your photographer wouldn't thank me if I returned you to him all scratches,' he smiled.

'He wouldn't,' she agreed dryly.

Luke shot her a quick glance. 'Don't you get on?'

'Not as well as he'd like,' she replied pointedly.

He shrugged cynically. 'I expect you know how to keep him in his place. How long have you been a model?'

'Since my parents died.' Paula saw no reason to lie over this. 'I had to do something,' her voice hardened in anger. 'They cared so much, they left me no money.'

Brief understanding touched the grey eyes regarding her shrewdly, but he merely remarked, 'That needn't be a hardship.'

'It depends on the circumstances, doesn't it?' she retorted sharply. 'I'm usually broke, and it's a drawback not having a proper career.'

'You're surely young enough to be able to train for one?' he frowned.

'But too lazy,' she laughed, thinking the conversation was getting over-serious. 'That's probably why I keep on modelling. In between jobs, I can at least do as I like.'

'Can't you choose to work with a photographer you like?' Luke enquired dryly. 'It can't be much fun working with one who wants to take you to bed all the time.'

Paula was too used to such frankness in the circles she moved in to be offended by it. She smiled coolly. 'It's not always as easy. I usually discover I have nothing left to pay the mortgage and have to take the first job that's available.'

'Like coming here?'

'Yes.'

'Well, why should I complain?' he grinned.

When Luke Armstrong smiled at her, Paula found herself smiling back involuntarily. It wasn't going to be difficult to get on with him, though what kind of a man he was, apart from being friendly and attentive, she had as yet to discover. He appeared to like her; if he hadn't, she suspected, there was no way by which she could have influenced him to have anything to do with her. It must also be a stroke of luck meeting him like this and she was determined to make the most of it.

'Do you live here all the time?' she asked, removing her sandals and trailing her pink-tipped toes in the white sand, as they wandered by the sea.

Luke strolled by her side, but after helping her safely on to the beach, down a steep incline, he made no further attempt to touch her. 'Most of the time,' he gazed into the distance, speaking absently.

'It's a beautiful island,' glancing at him quickly, Paula probed cautiously. 'But don't you get tired of it?'

'Sometimes I get tired of my own company,' he retorted.

Deliberately she gave the impression of talking idly. 'I suppose you could always sell it.'

Luke nodded. 'I often think of getting rid of it.'

'But you never do.'

He shrugged, his glance leaving the glittering blue ocean to return to the girl by his side. 'Maybe, like you, I enjoy being lazy.'

Paula bent to pick up a silvery shell and firmly stifled her growing curiosity. She thought, at this stage, it might be wiser not to ask too many questions which might arouse his suspicions. She couldn't believe he was lazy and she wondered how he passed the time, but, as she had already discovered, it might not take much to induce him to move, she forced herself to be content.

She kept to comments she believed an ordinary visitor might make. 'I've never been on a privately owned island before. How big is it?'

'About a mile long. It varies in width.'

'Are there many islands like this?'

'Thousands, scattered all over the Caribbean,' he replied briefly. 'A lot are just uninhabited rocks and reefs, of no use to anyone. Ones like this are being constantly sought after by developers.'

Paula was dismayed to find guilty colour creeping under her skin. She wasn't used to feeling embarrassed. Refusing to believe she could be, she laughed lightly, 'I imagine you've been approached by a few?'

'I've had offers, some I've been tempted to accept,' he confessed, his eyes swerving to the patch of jungle ahead of them. 'One of the snags attached to your so-called paradise island is the constant battle against nature.'

Better and better, Paula thought, while suggesting casually, 'You must find it handy for entertaining.'

'I rarely do much of that,' he retorted quite curtly. 'Those who do come here have to like slumming.'

'I wouldn't call it slumming exactly,' she grimaced, surprised at his tone and thinking of the breakfast she'd just had. 'You have servants and a lot to offer,' provocatively she paused before adding with a teasing glance, 'In the way of sea and sand.'

Luke laughed with obvious amusement. 'Everything palls eventually.'

Swiftly she retorted. 'Not the opinion of the ladies who visit you, surely?'

He grinned, countering smoothly, 'How do you think you'd like living here, now that you've seen it?'

'I'm not sure,' Paula replied slowly, avoiding his steady grey gaze as she remembered the role she was supposed to play. If she got the chance. If she was to persuade Luke to part with his island, it wouldn't do to pretend it was a place she would never want to leave.

Carefully, as he smiled slightly at her answer and walked on, she scrutinised his tall figure. Before breakfast he had discarded his shorts for a pair of fawn slacks and the black shirt he wore with them was open to the waist, which did nothing to hide a virility she found somewhat frightening. This man's obvious sexuality might be the worst thing she had to contend with, if the plan the Cranfords had devised was to succeed. She didn't think he was the type to force himself on a woman, but how could she tell? If she got him to agree to leave the island, might he not demand more proof than could be supplied by a few kisses that her promise to live with him afterwards would be fulfilled?

Paula swallowed a quiver of fear as he paused to wait for her. As she caught up she was aware of his eyes dwelling on her warmly. 'If my visitors were all like you,' he said huskily, 'I don't think I'd ever want them to leave.'

'I might take some convincing of that,' she smiled, forcing herself to glance at him flirtatiously again. Wouldn't it be better to find out now if she was capable of leading him on? In another few days it might be too late.

Hearing Luke draw a sharp breath, she steeled herself grimly for what she knew she was inviting. They were both opportunists, she thought bitterly. Luke intended satisfying a hunger which, because of his isolated position, might not have been appeased for weeks, while she was trying to find an answer to a question she shouldn't have needed to ask. But while she had a fairly clear idea of what lay behind Luke Armstrong's motives, it was unlikely that he knew anything of hers.

As his hand went to her waist and he slowly drew her closer, she wished, not for the first time, that she enjoyed this kind of thing. He didn't hurry, which seemed to imbue every movement he made with twice as much meaning. She made herself stand still as his arms slid around her. She even, like an act of defiance against her own frigidity, removed her sunglasses and let them drop on the sand. Conscious of his grin of male satisfaction, she had to clench her teeth to prevent herself from struggling from him hysterically. When her heart began beating wildly, she let him put it down to the impression he obviously believed he was making, rather than on her rising apprehension.

Carefully, as if seeking to reassure her, yet incite her even further, his hands explored her back, then ran lightly over her shoulders, his fingers tracing every hollow and curve with infinite patience. Then slowly, after a few minutes of just standing holding her, his head bent to allow his firm mouth to caress her smooth brow and close her wide, darkened eyes with feather-light kisses.

Paula had been kissed too many times before not to know exactly how she would react. Everything about her grew cold and froze, until she felt like a block of ice. She had grown tired of experimenting, it was always the same. This was why she had eventually been driven to accept Ian's proposal. He had affected her no differently from other men, but, with his wealth and prospects of a title, she had told herself she might as well settle for the best she could get.

With Luke Armstrong, her reactions were so identical to the ones she was familiar with that she wondered how she could ever have thought, when he had first taken her in his arms, that she might feel differently. After a moment, when nothing happened, she actually felt grateful. It would make everything easier if she could leave him one day, without a qualm, knowing she would have no regrets. Meanwhile, she rebuked herself, hadn't she better give him some encouragement? When he murmured thickly that she was beautiful, she laughed softly and wound her arms about his neck.

So far, he had caressed but not kissed her, other than making light forays over her forehead and cheeks. It wasn't until her bare, slender arms found their way around his neck that with a rough exclamation his mouth sought and found and covered hers.

Recovering from the first shiver of fright that rushed through her, Paula tried to respond. Obediently, under the expressive pressure of Luke's mouth, she parted her lips and pressed her slight body to the demanding hardness of his. Submissively she did her best to make him believe she enjoyed this kind of thing as much as he appeared to be doing. She continued pretending as his warm, moist lips explored her mouth and his breathing became laboured and uneven.

His low murmur of something approaching disgust seemed a clear indication that her response had not been as satisfying as she expected. When the pressure of his mouth gradually eased to break the contact, Paula remained motionless in his arms, gazing at him in bewilderment. In the last moment before he had stopped kissing her, red-hot blood had began pouring through her veins. She couldn't be sure, of course, and she had no wish to experiment further. It must have been a trick, due to the sun, perhaps, rather than Luke's overpowering masculinity.

All the same, it was with a gasp of very real fright that she wrenched herself away from him, not altogether convinced that nothing had happened to her. Yet, in the same seconds as it took to push him away, she was sickened to realise that if she wanted to attract him, she wasn't going the best way about it. Repulsing him wasn't going to achieve anything!

Swiftly she lowered thick lashes in order to hide the fear and disdain in her eyes. 'I'm sorry, Luke,' blindly she picked up her glasses, trying to sound both helpless and shattered, 'you took me by surprise . . .'

'I took myself by surprise.' With relief, Paula heard that his voice was ironic but gentle. 'I don't usually grab a girl I've just met and begin mauling her. I'm afraid I find you a terrible temptation.'

'Perhaps you're lonely?' Paula faltered.

'Sometimes I am,' he didn't deny it. 'But that's no excuse for losing control. It must be because you're so devastating . . .'

Because she had the distinct feeling of being teased, she returned his mocking smile cheekily. 'Even Miss Tucker had to sing for her supper.'

'If you're referring to your breakfast,' he laughed, 'I don't consider you owe me anything.'

'And the free use of your island,' she reminded him.

His mouth quirked while his eyes gleamed derisively. 'You provided some entertainment.'

'When you kissed me,' she asked, managing to sound indifferent, 'did you consider that in the same light?'

'No,' he frowned suddenly, 'Anyway, what's a few kisses?'

'They're all you're getting,' Paula retorted rashly, somehow hurt that he should dismiss them so casually.

'Don't be so sure,' he drawled, a wry twist of humour to the sensuous mouth that had sent such frissons of alarm through Paula only moments ago.

Finding it frustrating having to think each time before she spoke, she bit her lip uncertainly. If she was too emphatic over not seeing Luke—or kissing him again, it might make him very suspicious if she were to return here. When she didn't reply, he pressed a swift kiss on her lips, as if to confirm that he had had the last word, then grasping her hand with an air of superiority, he led her back up the cliff.

On the way, he didn't pursue their previous conversation or even talk much about anything else. Paula was glad of the chance to control her racing pulses and plan her next move. It wasn't easy, especially when she had no experience of this kind of thing to guide her. The Cranfords had been full of general advice but no help at all otherwise. She only knew she must be careful. Only a fool would underestimate Luke

Armstrong's intelligence. His casual manner, she sensed instinctively, hid a man far more astute than was immediately apparent. On the other hand, he was obviously as susceptible as most men to a pretty face, a point decidedly in her favour.

Luke saw them off after lunch, when Ron insisted on returning to Barbados. Paula resisted the temptation to ask if she would see him again. If he didn't seek her out, she must try and get in touch with him after the others had gone back to England. Some of her former confidence was fading. That Luke had enjoyed a few hours in her company didn't prove he wouldn't easily forget her once she was out of sight. When Lena and Coral teased that he had been unable to keep his eyes off her, she felt gratified but not wholly impressed.

Ron said at dinner that evening, 'Be wary of a man like Armstrong, Paula. He eats little girls like you for breakfast.'

'That cliché's worn out,' she retorted tartly.

'Maybe,' he admitted coldly, 'but it still applies.'

She laughed; sometimes she enjoyed provoking him. 'I've been dealing with men like him for years, Ron, and lost nothing yet.'

'If that's a hint that you're still as intact as the day you were born, I'm inclined to believe you,' he said sourly. 'You're a cool little customer, Paula. You've been thoroughly spoiled and you think the world owes you, yet in some ways you're totally naïve. You're so damned overflowing with confidence that one of these days you're bound to come a cropper, and don't ever say I didn't warn you.'

Paula glared at him. She was familiar with his opinion of her. Because she always rejected him, he was forever trying to set her down. He was vindictive and she hated him! It would be no penance to see the last of him! She was inclined to throw something, but instead said scornfully, 'I hardly think Mr Armstrong presents any great threat.'

Lena and Coral were listening. They were used to

hearing Ron insulting Paula, he never seemed to mind if he had an audience. 'I shouldn't care how dangerous Luke was if he took a fancy to me,' drawled Coral. 'Men like him are few and far between.'

Which might be just as well! Paula thought dryly, smiling gratefully at Mrs Hartley, who tactfully changed the subject. One Luke Armstrong would be enough for any girl, though she had no doubt whatsoever that she could manage him when the time came. It was the methods she might have to employ in order to persuade him to leave his island, rather than any misgivings over her ability to do it, that bothered her. When Luke had held her in his arms, that morning, she had been aware of something more than the usual ice in her veins. It still puzzled and vaguely alarmed her. Fearing it was something that might make her vulnerable and thus hinder her in some way, she had done her best to get to the bottom of it, but, as she slowly ate her dinner, she was forced to confess that she wasn't yet any nearer to understanding it.

Later that evening, when she received a phone call from England, she went almost eagerly to answer it. She was relieved to escape from Ron who, after tiring of baiting her, had began pestering her to go out with him. He had been so displeased when she refused that she had been forced to believe he would like an affair with her, as Luke had hinted. It had taken her quite a while to convince him she wasn't interested.

Her call was from Denis Cranford, who demanded to know why she hadn't a phone in her room. He had apparently discovered she would have to speak to him from one of the bubble-fronted boxes in the hotel foyer.

'As it happens, I'm sharing a room,' she retorted, 'so it wouldn't have made much difference.'

'After the others leave,' he snapped, 'make sure you have better facilities. Meanwhile, keep your voice down and be careful what you're saying.'

Not for the first time that day, Paula felt like telling someone where they could go to! Bitterly she thought of

the time when she hadn't felt forced to restrain herself.
Denis sounded happier when she told him what kind of
a day she'd had which, somehow, only made her feel
more depressed.

'You're doing better than I expected,' he said. 'You
haven't changed your mind?'

'No,' she replied, but so stiffly he must have caught a
hint of her continuing unease.

'I know you'll be sensible when you realise all you
have to gain,' his voice warmed over the line as he
hinted unmistakably that if all went well there might be
no limits to his generosity.

More convinced than ever that men were all the
same, Paula gazed cynically at the phone when he hung
up. Regarding doing what the Cranfords asked, she
acknowledged she was no better than they were. She
didn't want to do it, but she couldn't resist the money.
Hollowly she laughed. It was either Luke Armstrong's
island or her flat. She didn't have much choice, did she?

Luke came to the hotel the following evening and
stayed to dinner. Lena saw him first and hurried to
break the news.

'Luke's talking to the manager,' she said breathlessly.
'I'm sure it's him, though he's wearing a suit. If he's
here to see us, I must say he hasn't wasted much time!'

Paula didn't say anything. Ron stared at her
suspiciously and she guessed he was wondering if she
had arranged to see Luke again.

Coral threw her a resigned glance. 'Some people have
all the luck. He must have taken a fancy to you, Paula.
Aren't you feeling pleased with yourself?'

'He could be here for plenty of reasons other than
seeing me,' Paula said coldly. 'As he happens to live in
the area there must be heaps of people he knows.'

Yet when Luke approached the corner where they
were having pre-dinner drinks, she was aware of a small
surge of triumph. It increased as his eyes went swiftly
over their small group, then stayed on her. He made no
attempt to hide the fact that he was pleased to see her,

and she basked in the warmth of his smile. Whether she was committed to work for the Cranfords or not, everything was going her way. She hadn't thought it would be so easy.

'Good evening.' Tearing his eyes from Paula's spectacularly beautiful face, he addressed the company in general. 'Do you mind if I join you?'

The girls and Mrs Hartley welcomed him happily, but Ron merely grunted and muttered, 'I suppose we owe you?'

Recalling having used almost those exact words, Paula nearly blushed, but Luke didn't rise to the bait. Ignoring Ron, he ordered another round of drinks. Everyone asked for the same again, and when the waiter departed after bringing Paula a large orange juice, he raised expressive brows.

'Do you find abstinence good for the soul?' he asked mockingly.

'Not particularly.' She was rather startled to find Luke so quickly by her side, but managed to answer him demurely. 'I find it's easier to work without a muzzy head in the mornings.'

'Wise girl,' he grinned, his teeth very white against tanned skin.

She liked his white suit, the way it set off his tall figure. The width of his shoulders was impressive, as was the arrogant set of his head. She didn't recognise the peculiar sinking feeling in her stomach and dismissed it as hunger.

She was glad she was looking her best, this evening, as well. The attractive black chiffon creation she had chosen to wear was daringly cut and very sophisticated, just the thing to attract a man's attention and hold it. Her shoulders were bare and she had brushed her hair into a mass of golden-red curls to reveal the slender, inviting smoothness of her long neck. She had used some of her favourite French perfume from Van Cleef & Arpels of Paris, and clasped a hand-carved crystal pendant on a string of quartz, crystal and haematite

beads round her throat. Such ornaments, like her
diamond bracelet and Cartier wristlet watch, she had
never been able to bring herself to part with. She felt
rewarded for the care she had taken over her
appearance now, as Luke Armstrong's grey eyes went
over her admiringly.

It was nearly nine when they went in for dinner, and
afterwards they danced. Luke took Lena and Coral on
to the floor first, then he asked Paula. Paula felt oddly
impatient waiting for her turn. She did a couple of
numbers with Ron, but she didn't enjoy it. He held her
too closely with eyes full of malice. He had watched her
talking to Luke during dinner and she knew he resented
her apparent interest in the other man. She felt her
heart sink unhappily. He would give her a rough time
tomorrow. He might have forgiven her for repulsing his
advances if she hadn't so clearly preferred Luke
Armstrong.

When she danced with Luke their steps fitted so well
she was surprised. She was light on her feet, but she
moved in his arms as if they had been dancing together
for years. He compelled her to follow him, which she
did until she began feeling she was flowing into him,
somehow becoming a part of him.

'You're a wonderful dancer,' he murmured in her ear.
'You'd be even better if you learned to relax.'

She was startled that he was aware of something she
hadn't been conscious of herself. Not until he
mentioned it did she feel the familiar tension still in her
body. She didn't tell him it was woven into her
indelibly; her body's defence against predatory males
was an intricate part of her.

'I might have problems that won't let me relax,' she
replied lightly, seeking to conceal the truth from him as
she did from everyone.

Luke merely smiled. 'I refuse to believe a girl like you
can have any problems.'

'You'd be surprised,' she muttered darkly.

He shrugged dismissively. 'I would be if I thought

you were serious.' Holding her away from him, a flicker of amusement came to his eyes. 'I like your dress, what there is of it, anyway.' Taking his time, he examined it thoroughly, while Paula squirmed and blushed and tried to close the gap between them as his roving glance rested longer than was necessary on certain parts of her anatomy.

He laughed softly, misinterpreting her flushed reactions. 'Missed me, have you?' he murmured huskily against her hair, pulling her close again.

About to deny this, she was irritated to remember in time that she'd be wiser to nod. Luke's confidence bothered her. She made up her mind that it would do him no harm to have it dented. He appeared to believe he was the answer to every maiden's prayer! He wouldn't appreciate being made a fool of, but it might be good for him. It would make him realise he couldn't win every time. And why should she forfeit her future security because he owned an island he liked so little that, according to his own words, he had often considered parting with it? When she went to stay with him, she would merely be accelerating a process he had already decided to put in action.

'It's regrettable that you have to return to England,' he said, one of his hands moving sensuously on her shoulder-blades. 'I should have enjoyed getting to know you better.'

His hand was demonstrating how, and Paula bit her lip uncertainly. She wished she had learnt how to flirt naturally with men instead of perfecting the art of keeping them at a distance. Did he mean he was resigned to her leaving and prepared to forget about her? She almost panicked as she saw the remuneration the Cranfords had offered being whipped away from her.

'We—I mean, I still have a day or two,' deliberately she smiled up into his eyes, not finding it nearly as difficult as she'd thought it would be.

'Great,' the grey eyes lightened appreciably as he

swung her from the terrace on which they were dancing to the deeper shadows beyond. 'Let's go for another walk beside the sea,' he suggested. 'I enjoyed our last one so much I've a fancy to repeat it.'

Paula wasn't sure which part of their walk he was referring to, but she was soon enlightened when he paused as soon as the sea lapped their feet and began kissing her.

He held her against him, his fingers caressing the back of her head while she felt his mouth lightly brushing hers. They stood like that for several seconds, her body pressed to his, and neither moved. The contact filled her with emotions too deep to understand and she couldn't be certain whether the pounding heartbeats she seemed to hear in her ears were his or her own. Then, as he deepened the kiss, there was that mixture of fire and ice in her veins, so new and frightening that she tried not to think beyond what he was doing to her, but, despite this, she stiffened.

'No?' Luke paused, his hand lingering on the curve of her breast although his arms slackened. His eyes were intent on her face, pale with the alarm she wasn't able to hide. 'I'm going too fast for you. Is that it?'

'Yes,' she whispered helplessly.

He laughed softly without taking offence. 'You like being wooed properly?'

Paula made an effort to pull herself together. 'I'm acting like a teenager on her first date!'

Smiling at her tenderly, Luke said, 'I don't think you've had a lot of experience, but we don't have much time.'

'For—what?' she couldn't help asking.

'Who knows?' he replied enigmatically, drawing her under the concealing fronds of a giant palm.

Tension mounted in Paula again. He was being patient with her, but she could feel his determination to have his own way as she stiffened against the gentle persuasion of his hand. 'Luke,' she entreated, 'can't you wait?'

He stopped so suddenly she half fell against him. 'For—what?' he asked, as she had done, but with a teasing note in his voice. 'All I was seeking was a quiet spot to tell you how beautiful you are.'

Involuntarily she giggled. 'You already have.'

'Ah,' he smiled, 'but some things can stand repeating, and that would only be a start. As well as a beautiful face, you have a wonderful body. I'm trying to find words to describe it, but you're not giving me much encouragement.'

Paula swallowed. He was teasing, of course. 'We've only known each other a few hours,' she protested.

'I've made love to a woman knowing her less,' he drawled.

Sensing he was taunting her deliberately, Paula stared at him reprovingly. 'Are you trying to shock me?'

He laughed outright. 'How did you guess?'

'It wasn't difficult.'

Coaxingly he cupped her chin in his hand. 'I was only after your co-operation.'

'Not for what you have in mind!'

She refused to smile at him, but her quick tongue appeared to amuse him. Whimsically he smoothed her hot cheek with his thumb. 'How can you tell what I have in mind, lady?'

'What all men usually have . . .'

'Do I detect a note of cynicism?' he broke in, drawing her almost roughly to him. His face sobered as he muttered, 'You don't have to fear my intentions, sweetheart. I won't deny that I'd like to undress you slowly and take you to bed with me. I'd like to make love to you until you had no breath left to deny me, but I'll do none of these things without your permission.'

Why did some strange premonition whisper that these were words he would one day remember bitterly? 'No one speaks to me like that!' she retorted angrily.

'Then it's maybe about time someone did,' he retorted darkly, stilling her struggles and commanding starkly, 'Kiss me.'

With the reason for her being here so constantly on her mind, Paula felt compelled to obey. Obediently she raised her mouth to allow the warm moist invasion of his. She tried not to think of anything, though his kisses were too shattering not to alarm her, and a peculiar ache in her body deepened until it was almost a pain.

'Let me go!' she moaned, unable to bear it any longer.

'Stop fighting me,' whispered Luke, as she pleaded against his lips. 'Why can't you relax?'

'Because—I can't . . .'

'Don't be foolish!'

The urgent throb behind his words came to her, filling her with an excitement that swiftly smothered her alarm. For a breathless instant she felt dizzy and weak at the knees. Feebly she fought to escape the increasing pressure of his arms. She knew she had to stop him, but she felt completely helpless. He was holding her tightly with one hand, the other slid down her spine with tormenting slowness from her neck to her waist. The quality of his caresses paralysed her. Every time his hands moved they seemed to find more sensitive spots, while the hot kisses he pressed on her protesting mouth aroused her to near-hysteria. Sanity seemed to abandon her as she became captive to a force so powerful she could do nothing but surrender. Far from being full of ice, her body began threatening to burn her up.

Suddenly, to her stunned surprise, Luke thrust her from him with a bitten-off oath, instead of lowering her to the sands as she had feared. 'We'd better get back to the hotel,' he rasped, 'if I'm to keep the promise I made you.'

Paula stared at him uncomprehendingly, still confused by the magnitude of feeling he had built up inside her. It must be hate, she assured herself dazedly.

As they retraced their footsteps, he asked in a voice that still sounded husky, 'How do you like the hotel?'

'It's all right,' she replied indifferently, 'but no different from thousands of others.'

'I thought you would be enthralled with it,' he glanced at her dryly. 'Women usually are—it's five-star.'

Paula thought of the number of similar places she had stayed in with her parents, and frowned. Top hotels had always appealed to her greatly, she couldn't understand why they didn't now. She avoided answering directly, because she couldn't explain even to herself.

'When my parents were alive,' she replied evasively, 'we had a house in the country and I liked going there. The neighbours all had children who——' she laughed as she remembered, 'nearly drove my mother mad! I adored them, though, perhaps because I'm an only child. When I grew up I was going to have at least half a dozen of my own. That was before I discovered they weren't found under gooseberry bushes.'

Luke laughed. 'I always believed the stork brought them.'

'Have you any children, Luke?' she ventured. The Cranfords said he wasn't married, but he might have been, for all they knew.

'I've never been that careless,' he said, making her flush.

'I wondered if you'd been divorced,' she floundered. 'I realise you aren't married now.'

'How can you be so sure?' he frowned.

Paula blessed her stupid tongue. 'I—I suppose I just took it for granted.'

'Because I kissed you?'

When she nodded numbly, he said sternly, 'I'm not married, but I could have been. You should be careful, in future.'

How many strange men did he think she went out with? Recovering her poise, she made a small face at him. 'Thanks—I'll remember!'

'You'd better!' he growled.

As they reached the terrace again, Paula told herself she really should be careful, if not in the way Luke implied. What on earth had made her start on about liking children? That was one bit of information she believed in keeping to herself. The trouble with Luke Armstrong was, he was too easy to talk to. The strange kind of rapport between them might make the job she had to do easier in one sense, but it also had its dangers. She would need to be constantly on guard against blurting out bits of information it might be better he didn't know about.

An hour later, as Luke was leaving, she asked, with apparent anxiety, if he would be coming back again while she was here. Yesterday, when she left his island, she hadn't mentioned the possibility of seeing him again, but now she believed it might be a good move to give him the impression that it was important to her that she did.

'I'm coming over tomorrow.' Taking her hand, he held it gently, a smile on his hard, handsome face.

Paula returned his smile, although it wavered as he carried her hand to his lips. 'I'll look out for you,' she promised softly.

'Be sure you do,' he said quietly, staring straight into her eyes.

## CHAPTER THREE

RON was in one of his worst moods the following morning. It hadn't pleased him to see Paula returning from the beach the previous evening, holding Luke's hand. He hadn't liked the way Luke had continued to dance with her either. He had wrapped her closely in his arms and taken no notice of Ron's stony glances, though he had seemed driven to warn her, half teasingly, that because of the way Ron was looking at her, it might pay her to keep her bedroom door locked.

'I'm sharing with Mrs Hartley,' Paula had replied.

'Good,' he had smiled, but with obvious relief that she wouldn't be in danger of suffering Ron's unwelcome advances. Mrs Hartley was a formidable lady, with years of experience of dealing with over-amorous cameramen.

The morning's work having been silently acknowledged a disaster, the team went out again after lunch. Ron's mood continued to be foul. Mrs Hartley had a word with him about it, but it didn't improve. He shouted at Coral until she burst into tears, and, as the oldest of the three girls, she had six years' modelling experience behind her. Without apologising, he ordered her to retire until she got herself sorted out and learned to do things properly.

Then he started on the unfortunate Lena. When Paula's turn came, she was startled yet relieved to find Luke Armstrong standing watching them. She wondered how long he had been there and how he had found them. The manager of the hotel must have told him where they might be working.

Surprisingly, instead of telling him to get lost, Ron stopped scowling and invited Luke amiably to help out with a few scenes. 'Background interest only,' he grinned, when Luke looked doubtful.

'Providing that's all it is,' Luke warned him.

Paula listened with mixed feelings to this exchange between the two men. Ron had been quick to realise that Luke would make splendid background material, the kind guaranteed to make women readers of the magazine they were working for look twice at any page he was on. Ron's professionalism was triumphing over the darker side of his nature, but she didn't trust him. She wished Luke had refused.

Ron, an innocent grin glued on his face, asked Luke if he would be kind enough to remove his shirt and lean against the tree directly behind Paula. Luke duly obliged, and Paula found herself watching as closely as Lena and Coral as he slowly unbuttoned his shirt and peeled it over his broad shoulders.

'The girls are enjoying the show,' Ron leered sarcastically. 'They've never seen a real live man before.'

Luke grinned carelessly. 'I can stand a little admiration, it won't go to my head.'

'Oh, let's get on with it!' snapped Paula, just about ready to explode. She had been standing round in the sun all day; she felt too weary to appreciate humour of any kind. She had looked forward to seeing Luke this evening, not when she was so hot and fed-up that she might be in danger of throwing something at him and spoiling everything.

She had reckoned without Luke's astuteness, though. If Ron had mischief in mind, he humoured him but refused to go along with it. He did pose, but only twice, and both times kept well back. Even so, Paula considered he was much too near. She could feel his eyes on her each time she moved, and some of the bikinis she wore seemed no more than two pieces of string. Long before they had finished her whole body was so over-heated she might have had a fever, and she knew it wasn't due to the sun.

She rode back to the hotel with Luke in the car he had borrowed. 'I didn't think you'd be here this early,' she muttered, conscious of the sullen note in her voice.

'I had an appointment,' he smiled, 'that's why.'

'Oh,' Paula coloured slightly. She had thought he couldn't wait to see her. 'How do you travel from your island?' she asked quickly. 'You must have a boat?'

'A small one.'

Impatiently she brushed back a tangle of red-gold curls. 'It's nice to see you, but I wish you'd waited at the hotel,' she said crossly. 'I consider Ron took advantage of you.'

He laughed softly, his eyes slanting pointedly to her small thrusting breasts. 'I had the advantage, I think.'

Knowing what he meant, she deliberately chose to pretend she didn't. How dared he! she smouldered, her body tingling so much she had to turn away from him. 'I'm sure you can't enjoy the thought of being splashed all over a London magazine.'

'I've nothing to hide,' Luke said indifferently.

When the colour in her cheeks deepened, he obviously mistook her guilt for anger. 'Come on, sweetheart,' he coaxed, 'if I hadn't stepped in you might never have survived. You saw what the swine did to your two friends.'

She gulped. 'So that was why you did it?'

'You don't imagine I didn't need a powerful incentive,' he shrugged. 'Now are you ready to stop grousing and say thank you?'

Paula felt ashamed yet oddly triumphant. She hadn't thought Luke cared so much. Running her fingers gently down his arm, she circled his wrist, then warmly squeezed his hand. 'I'm sorry,' she whispered.

'That's a double bonus,' he whispered back.

Glancing at him quickly, she was surprised to see a tinge of red creeping under his jaw. She drew a sharp breath, this time distinctly uneasy. Something was always trying to warn her that Luke Armstrong was an unknown quantity, that he wasn't totally the mild-mannered man she was becoming used to. She suspected he had a temper from the way his mouth sometimes went and the set of his head, but she was sure there wasn't anything to really alarm her.

'How much longer will you be here?' he asked abruptly.

'I'm still not sure,' she shrugged.

'I'd like to come and see you off,' he said, explaining why he was enquiring.

'I hate airport goodbyes,' she mumbled, hoping this might deter him. It would be difficult to engineer a row with Ron with Luke looking on. If Luke did turn up she would have to pretend she had changed her mind over going back—just like that, but a row with Ron, especially when Luke knew what kind of a man he was, might remove any suspicion that she was staying behind deliberately.

At the hotel, Luke asked if she would have dinner with him, somewhere else on the island.

'I'd like that,' Paula agreed. 'But you'll have to give me an hour or two. I was up at six and I'd like a rest and shower.'

'That's okay,' he smiled gently. 'I want to see someone anyway. I'll pick you up at seven.' As she left him, he called after her, 'Don't dress up. I have a tie on the boat, but that's about all!'

After a rest it took Paula almost an hour to get ready. She had a long bath, then washed her hair, which took quite a time to restore to order. After smoothing on body lotion, she painted her finger and toenails a delicate shade to match her lipstick and had to wait for them to dry. She had a wrap-and-tie dress in white cotton she had decided to wear and she didn't want nail varnish all over that!

Mrs Hartley chatted to her while she was waiting, but she didn't take much notice. Mrs Hartley's husband had apparently got himself involved with a young girl of only nineteen.

'Why not divorce him?' Paula suggested impatiently.

Mrs Hartley went pale. 'Oh, I couldn't do that!' she faltered. 'He might come to his senses?'

'You'd be better off without him,' Paula retorted sharply. 'He'll only do it again.'

'But I love him!' Mrs Hartley wailed.

'Love!' Paula scorned. 'Take it from me, there's no such thing!'

'I'd die without him!'

How stupid could one get? She felt ashamed of her sex. Staring at Mrs Hartley's anguished face, Paula realised it would be a waste of time arguing with her. Her husband was enjoying himself with a girl less than half her age and all she could think of was getting him back! It was beyond Paula's comprehension.

'Have you packed, dear?' Mrs Hartley, looking somewhat defenceless, was obviously wishing she had kept her grievances to herself. 'It suddenly occurred to me that you might have forgotten, and you know we always catch an early plane.'

'I'll do it later,' Paula pretended she hadn't been sure. 'Ron might change his mind.'

'No, I've just talked to him,' Mrs Hartley replied. 'This afternoon's shots couldn't be better. I've seen the first rushes and they're all we need.'

'Good,' said Paula, reaching for her dress. She hoped Luke would never learn that she had deliberately deceived him or there might be hell to pay! She felt nervous already. Did Mrs Hartley think she was the only one with problems? She had to get through tomorrow and there was still this evening. Whatever happened she must get rid of Luke after dinner, or as soon as possible.

When Luke told her he was taking her sailing, she could have screamed in frustration. She was certain she must warrant an Oscar for the delighted smile she produced.

'There's a moon. I thought it would appeal to you,' he grinned. 'It will be most romantic.'

'You think of everything, Luke,' she murmured humbly, cursing under her breath. 'I didn't think men like you existed.'

'You really ought to consider changing your job,' he frowned, real concern in his eyes. 'What you're doing now may seem glamorous, but you're bound to meet all the wrong kind of men.'

'I think I'm just about ready to take your advice.' Because she was still mad with him, she decided to string him along. Glancing at him wistfully, she sighed, 'I wish you'd been around when my parents died.'

'Poor darling,' Luke said softly, clearly not suspecting the sarcasm she concealed. 'But it's not too late, I'm here now. How long is it since your parents died?'

Paula thought fast. 'Four years.' If she wanted his sympathy, that sounded better than eight months.

'You were only a child.'

'N-nearly eighteen.'

'You poor kid!' his voice deepened with remorse. 'I'm sorry I was so rough the other day. I didn't realise.'

Paula suppressed a cat-like purr. Poor kid, indeed! Soon she'd have him eating out of her hand. Men were all alike—they prided themselves on their superior intelligence while any half-witted woman could make a fool of them. Yet, as her temper subsided, she felt a twinge of disquiet. She might have had a chequered career, but she had always made a point of sticking to the truth. Having to resort to lies because of her commitments to the Cranfords was easier than she had thought it might be, but, strangely enough, she was discovering it was doing nothing for the pride she had always had in her own integrity. The sooner this job was over, the better she would like it, she told herself unhappily.

Luke's boat, which they reached by dinghy, was a medium-sized cabin cruiser, well appointed but, like his house, fairly basic. Paula would rather have dined at the hotel.

'Done any sailing?' asked Luke casually, as he helped her aboard.

'Not really,' she answered evasively. What sailing she had done had been confined to the huge yachts belonging to her father's friends. Perhaps once a year, Paula had joined her parents to go cruising in the

Mediterranean or around the Greek islands with some millionaire or another. Luke wouldn't be impressed by that kind of sailing. 'I suppose I could learn,' she said carelessly.

'I'd be a hard taskmaster,' he grinned, and she shivered as somehow his words had a prophetic ring.

'How many slaves do you have?' she forced herself to grin back.

'None at the moment.' He led her down to the galley. It was neat and clean. She noticed a lot of packages lying around.

'Aren't we going anywhere?' she asked with a frown, as he began to get busy. 'On the boat, I mean.'

'There's dinner to cook,' he shook his head. 'I think we'll just stay where we are.'

This suited Paula, though she didn't say so. 'What culinary delights are you planning?' she teased lightly as he threw off his jacket.

'Steak and salad,' he replied briefly, pausing as his eyes travelled over her intently, reminding her of the afternoon. 'This contraption,' he waved a hand towards the stove, 'has its limitations, but it does steak real good.'

Paula slanted it a suspicious glance. 'Do you expect me to do the cooking?'

He smiled at her doubtful expression. 'Let's do it together. Sharing's always more fun.'

Her doubtful gaze transferred to her dress. Reading it exactly, Luke said reassuringly, 'You look beautiful in that, and I promise it will be the same pristine white when you leave. Would you rather take it off or have a pinny?'

'The latter will do,' she replied stiffly, trying to enter into the spirit of things but failing dismally. She suspected Luke was teasing her, but she had never been very good at this kind of male and female sparring. Luke was good company, he warmed something inside her, but it was actually this natural relaxing of her usual reserve that made her wary. 'If I'd known this was the

kind of thing you were planning,' she said, 'I'd have
tried to borrow some jeans, but I've nothing like that
with me.'

As he sought for something to cover her up, she
watched him with an unconscious frown. It wasn't her
own feelings she should be considering but Luke's. He
had given some indication that he would miss her, but
not a lot. Hadn't he even offered to see her off? If she
hadn't been so busy assessing the nuisance value of
that, the real point of his offer might not have escaped
her. If Luke was so willing to say goodbye to her then
she couldn't have made a very deep impression. Because
he had kissed her once or twice, she had believed he was
falling for her, when who should know better than she
just how little meaning there could be in a few kisses.
All the time she had been so busy pondering her own
various reactions, she hadn't seriously considered his.
Instead of taking it for granted that he was attracted,
she should have realised she had nothing concrete to go
on. Nothing had been definitely achieved and she might
only have a few more hours to work on him.

Work on him! Suddenly she hated such a vulgar
expression. Almost as much as she hated an unkind fate
that had forced her into such a situation. As her throat
thickened with tears of self-pity, she swallowed them
bitterly. It was no good feeling sorry for herself. Hadn't
she told herself a thousand times lately that self-pity
would get her nowhere? The fact remained that she had
only what was left of the evening to make sure that
Luke's feelings for her deepened to the extent that when
he discovered she hadn't returned to England, he would
care enough to invite her to stay on his island.

At the same time, she must take care not to flirt with
him too much, so that he was sated and lost interest.
Her soft mouth twisted wryly. Never having let a man
make love to her, she couldn't see herself leading Luke
on as far as that. All she probably need do was to
encourage him a little. If she was clever about it, it
might never be necessary to go much further.

Luke found an apron at last with a grunt of masculine impatience. 'Rose tidies up here occasionally, which means it's always weeks before I can find anything again.'

Paula experienced a tiny flicker of alarm. 'Who—is Rose?'

Luke closed the drawer he had turned upside down with a bang. 'Remember, she cooked your breakfast and lunch.'

'Oh, your servant!' Paula was so relieved she forgot to be sophisticated for a moment and laughed.

Shaking out the apron, Luke tied it around her himself. 'Your waist is incredible,' he sighed. 'This afternoon, I thought it the smallest I'd ever seen. It took me all my time to keep my hands off you. Do you realise some of that swimwear you were wearing scarcely covered your breasts?'

Such frankness, from Luke, did peculiar things to Paula's breathing. 'You might be interested to learn,' she told him evasively, 'that swimwear is from a leading designer and costs the earth in shops.'

He grinned. 'I imagine it's the provocation women pay for, not the yardage of material?'

'You didn't have to look,' she almost added—'as hard,' but decided against it.

'I enjoyed it,' he quipped lightly, slipping the top of the apron around her neck, carefully lifting a mass of curls to do so. 'Is this colour real?' he asked huskily, burying his face in them.

'Yes,' she gulped, as Luke turned her, with one of the fluid movements she was getting used to, into his arms.

Why did her heart quicken as though he had pressed a button to speed it up? She could feel the hard length of his powerful body against her, giving her a rather frightening impression of his strength. His warm breath fanned her face as he pulled her closer and let his ardent mouth close her eyes.

'If you want dinner,' she spoke carefully so her voice didn't wobble, 'you'd better let me get on with it.'

'I don't want to.'

'Luke!'

'Oh, all right,' he let her go with a rueful gleam in his eyes, 'you win—this time.'

Attempting to hide her hot cheeks, Paula busied herself with the steak, trying not to betray a lack of interest in what she was doing. Her cookery skills hadn't been tested until these last few months, she certainly hadn't tried them out on anyone but herself. She ate a lot of steak, for she had a healthy appetite that had to be satisfied with due regard to her weight.

'Will you do the salad?' she asked Luke, unable to bear the way he was watching her. 'First, though,' she gestured to the stove, 'I'd appreciate if you'd show me how this thing works?'

He laughed, moving her aside to manipulate the gas and put a match under the grill. 'If you've been on sailing trips before, you haven't been employed in the galley,' he teased.

'I'm not sure I like the sound of that!' she retorted, the cynical inflection in his voice annoying her against her will.

Meeting her resentful glance without noticeable remorse, he shrugged. 'I'm only jumping to the conclusions most people would come to.'

'Well, you're wrong!' she exclaimed. 'If you think . . .'

'Sometimes I think you're just a misguided, mixed-up kid, despite the sophistication,' he interrupted, bending his tall head to murmur mockingly against her ear.

She drew back sharply, alarmed by the sensation that shot through her again as his mouth touched her skin. 'I suppose I seem that way to you,' she snapped, 'at your great age!'

'Thirty-four?'

Paula bit her lip at the taunting glint in his eye. He was just in his prime and he knew it. Mutinously she rubbed her ear, surprised that it still tingled. Luke had such a shrewd, quick intelligence that she found it difficult to believe he was content to vegetate on a desert island.

'Luke,' she exclaimed, for a moment forgetting everything but her own curiosity, 'what do you do, exactly?'

'As little as possible,' he drawled.

So he refused to be drawn. Paula frowned at him in irritation. She felt hurt, too, that he had no wish to confide in her. 'You don't strike me as being lazy.'

'In certain situations,' he grinned, 'I'm not. Haven't I pursued you unremittingly?'

Her mouth tightened impatiently and she was determined to beat him at his own game. 'You pretend to be fond of women, yet you live alone.'

'From choice,' he shrugged, 'but that doesn't mean I have to deprive myself.'

She could guess what that meant! Luke might live by himself on an island, but the mainland wasn't far away. Here, on Barbados, plenty of women would find time for a man like him. Paula felt a twinge of something absurdly like jealousy, so new to her that she paused a moment to examine it, even as she rejected it.

'This conversation is pointless,' she said coldly, turning her attention to the steak again. Requiring some seasoning, she began searching through the cupboards without asking permission, but couldn't find any. 'I want to make a sauce,' she explained, when Luke asked dryly what she was looking for.

'Rose and Henry usually see to things like that,' he replied.

'Well, they've slipped up this time.'

'Here, let me see.' Amused by her crossness, he reached adroitly past her into a small compartment. 'Is this what you're after?' He handed her a box of spices. As she nodded and began selecting what she needed, he teased with a smile, 'My mouth is beginning to water already!'

She hoped he wasn't going to be disappointed. She had a vague idea what went into certain things, but no great experience. 'Rose and Henry certainly look after you.' Passing back the box, she glanced at the well stocked cupboards. 'Do you use your boat often?'

'Occasionally I go off for a day or two, but I never need the half of what Rose packs,' he bent to kiss the tip of her nose. 'Like most women, she enjoys making a fuss.'

'You mean fussing over a man?'

He grinned, with a regrettable lack of disapproval. 'It's always nice to know someone cares.'

Paula threw him a wry glance as she stirred and blended, albeit not very professionally. 'It's a nice feeling, I agree, if you can get it.'

Luke laughed, his grey eyes teasing as he wrapped an arm around her cajolingly. 'Come up on deck, honey, and let me convince you, you aren't alone in the world. Leave the steak a moment.'

'What,' she objected shakily, 'and spoil it? And it's nearly nine o'clock!'

Luke's mouth quirked as he obviously tried to draw some conclusions from what she was saying. 'Perhaps you're right,' he agreed. 'Why ruin good food when we can talk and watch the moon later?'

The steak turned out less than well and Luke's praise surprised her. 'I haven't got the sauce quite right,' she contemplated it doubtfully. 'I guess I'm no cook.'

'I don't know.' Cutting off a bit of burnt meat, he chewed it with what looked very like determination. 'It certainly tastes different. You only need practice.'

Paula was about to scorn such a suggestion when she changed her mind. She might have made a big mistake. If Luke was one of those men whose heart could only be reached through his stomach, it wouldn't do much for her chances if she confessed she had no intention of trying to improve her cooking. 'I never get much opportunity,' she said instead, letting her voice trail off pathetically.

Glancing at her quickly, Luke refilled her glass. 'Drink up and cheer up,' he grinned. 'You never know what tomorrow might bring.'

A shiver of apprehension ran through her, making her fingers clutch nervously around her glass. Luke spoke idly and the warmth in his eyes seemed to deny that she was in any danger, so why did she feel she was standing on the edge of a volcano about to erupt? Recklessly she lifted the potent wine to her lips, taking a long drink, feeling she needed it.

'That's not your usual orange juice,' he warned, as she emptied the glass. 'I didn't expect you to take my advice quite so literally.'

'It won't do me any harm for once,' she said lightly, collecting their empty plates.

'Have I told you how good you look in that dress?' he said softly, as they finished off with fruit and cheese. 'The colour suits you. I'm glad you hadn't any jeans.'

'You told me before.'

He laughed as she frowned. 'That's not the kind of reply you should make,' he teased. 'You should smile and flutter those ridiculously long lashes of yours and look flattered.' The humour died from his eyes as his glance sharpened intently on her face. 'When I first saw you, Paula, I thought you were the most beautiful woman I'd ever seen, and I haven't changed my mind.'

Paula said slowly, as colour crept under her pale skin, 'You must have seen many beautiful women, Luke, and they've maybe all appealed to you. With some men it's a rare painting, or the business or property they would like to own.'

Luke leant over to press a lingering kiss on her full mouth. 'I'm not sure what you're trying to point out to me, sweetheart, but I assure you I don't regard you as one of those inanimate things. You're flesh and blood and therefore much more exciting. Now, are you ready for coffee?'

The coffee he made, with due regard for the slightly inebriated giggle Paula gave at his abrupt return to practicalities, was black and hot, and he dragged her up on deck to drink it. They drank it watching the stars and moon illuminating a wide path across the water. It was a wonderful night, the air warm and scented, playing insidiously on the senses. Paula felt hers stirring

as Luke put aside their empty cups and took her in his
arms, but he only held her close, not kissing her
immediately.

'Happy?' he asked, his chin resting on the top of her
head as he pulled her against him.

'I think so,' she sighed.

'Yes and no, you mean?'

'Don't let's talk about it,' she pleaded. 'I'm not sure
how I feel. You have me all at sea. I've never felt like
this before, so I can't explain it.'

She must have struck the right note unintentionally,
for his mouth curved against her brow with satisfaction.
'Do you know,' he confessed ironically, 'with any other
girl I wouldn't have been sitting here admiring the
moon. Not with a very comfortable bunk down below.'

'Oh, Luke,' she whispered, surprised at how naturally
she was acting. She wasn't even having to try hard.

He must have responded to something in her voice
she wasn't aware of, because he turned her to him,
inserting his fingers under her chin with a groan. 'You
go to my head,' he said huskily, his firm lips descending
as he raised her mouth so he might find it easily.

Instinctively, Paula tried to push him away, as all her
old fears swept down on her like an avalanche. Ignoring
her fluttering, protesting hands, his mouth began
invading hers in an exploratory kiss that made her
senses swim in rising panic.

She had never been kissed like this before. She felt
she had been removed from the sane earth she knew
and hurled to another planet—one like Mars, with
soaring uncontrollable temperatures. The burning
pressure of Luke's embrace was igniting a fire inside her
that threatened her rationality. There was no release or
pleasure. She was just a cauldron of seething,
unrecognisable emotions that frightened her. She
couldn't contain the sensations shooting through her,
and Luke had apparently no intention of having mercy
on her. The more she gasped frantically, the more
ruthlessly he held her against him while his mouth

plundered her shaking lips with devastating thoroughness. He seemed to be consumed by a hunger that was proving insatiable. When his hands slipped through the front of her dress to possess the rounded curves of her breasts, she was sure she was dissolving.

Yet, when the grinding pressure of his mouth finally eased, the protective tension faded from her limbs so she went soft against him. Praying he wouldn't renew his assault on her, she placed tentative fingers to her swollen lips, where the broken skin clearly revealed the rawness of Luke's needs. Even though his mouth had left hers, she was conscious of the hardness of his body pulsing closely over her own and the ache of desire in his eyes.

Still staring at her, he moved carefully from her with a wry shrug. 'It might be a good idea to take a cooling dive over the side, but on second thoughts, we might be wiser to go back ashore and take a long drive.'

'A—drive?' she breathed unevenly. 'What time is it?'

'Only eleven.'

'Late enough,' she insisted in a stronger voice, believing she might not be safe with him much longer— anywhere! 'I think it might be better if I tidied your galley and we went straight back to the hotel. I expect I'll be on early call.'

He appeared to connect the colour creeping under her skin with their lovemaking, rather than the guilt she was experiencing at giving the false impression that, for her, tomorrow would be just another working day.

'Forget the galley,' he said, as she edged away from him to go below. 'Rose will see to it.'

Paula nodded, but let a doubtful glance accompany the affirmative she gave. She'd had no intention of doing the dishes, but she guessed Luke would think none the less of her if she offered. She was only concerned with getting back to the hotel as soon as possible, now that she knew Luke was definitely attracted. The way in which he had kissed her, and a certain tautness in his manner since, assured her she wasn't mistaken. He wouldn't be displeased when he discovered she was still at the hotel after the others had left. Of this she was almost certain.

After wakening early, Paula rose and did her packing. Coffee was served in their rooms, but they would have breakfast on the plane. On the way to the airport, no one talked much. It was a beautiful morning, the kind of morning made for pleasure rather than work. Regret at having to leave it was expressed on all their faces. It would have been lovely to have gone for a swim and then lie around in the sun. That they mostly had other jobs waiting and couldn't have afforded to stay on at the five-star hotel anyway filled them all with bitter resignation. Once back in London, Barbados would soon be forgotten. It was leaving it that was the wrench.

Paula almost sighed with relief that there was no sign of Luke. Somehow, perhaps because he knew the manager of the hotel, she had suspected he might get wind of what was going on and turn up. The whole way to the airport, she had kept her fingers crossed and tried to act coolly in a situation that was playing havoc with her nerves.

Timing was important, and she was terrified of making a mistake. Wondering why most of her self-possession had deserted her, she waited until everyone was ready to board the plane before announcing suddenly. 'I'm not going home. I've decided to have a break for a few weeks.'

'Don't be so damned stupid!' exploded Ron, as the others looked at her with varying degrees of surprise. 'You're always complaining of being broke. Do you realise how much staying here is going to cost you?'

'I'll manage,' she said haughtily.

Ron drew a deep breath that obviously did nothing for him. 'You must be out of your tiny little mind!'

She stared at him balefully. It occurred to her that Ron and she were actually quarrelling; she needn't have worried about making it up. 'What's on my mind is none of your damned business!' she snapped.

Mrs Hartley interceded hurriedly, a worried frown on her face. 'Paula, are you sure you're doing the right thing? You must realise the agency won't be pleased if you don't return with us. You've let them down a lot lately, and they haven't unending patience.'

Only Coral and Lena accepted her decision to stay behind without protesting. They merely shrugged and said, 'See you,' then moved into the plane.

Ron muttered truculently. 'What the hell! If you're determined to go there, why should I care?'

Mrs Hartley spoke anxiously. 'Paula! Did you hear what I said?'

'Yes, but I'm not listening,' Paula smiled faintly, hoping Mrs Hartley understood she had no quarrel with her. Mrs Hartley might have done, for her eyes softened anxiously as they rested on Paula's hot face. Then, after a long hesitation, she sighed and followed the other girls.

His expression changed, Ron caught Paula's arm. 'Paula?'

'No!' she broke in firmly, before he could begin to plead. 'It's no use saying anything more, Ron. I've made up my mind.'

'Suit yourself, then,' he retorted harshly, flinging her arm away, then coming closer again, so she could see the venom in his eyes. 'You don't think I don't know what's really going on, do you? But when Luke Armstrong tires of you don't come running to me. You won't listen when I tell you he's like nothing you've ever experienced before, but believe me, my so smart but innocent little Paula, you're in for the shock of your life!'

Paula had to go and get herself a cup of coffee after the plane went—after that. Ron's words had shaken her more than she cared to admit. She had a very nasty taste in her mouth.

It took two cups of coffee before she felt able to look around for a taxi to take her back to the hotel. Before leaving the airport she remembered to act on Denis

Cranford's instructions again. Calling the hotel, she explained who she was, and that she had decided to stay on for a few days, and she asked if her old room or one similar was avilable. On hearing that one was, she sighed with relief. If the hotel hadn't been able to take her, this might have led to further complications, such as having to waste time trying to book into somewhere near to it and perhaps missing Luke.

# CHAPTER FOUR

THE first thing Paula did on returning to the hotel was to take a leisurely bath. Then she went to bed and slept for a few hours. When she woke it was noon, and she dressed slowly before going down to lunch. She thought of Luke as little as possible. Each time he crossed her mind she thrust his image from her. The only way she might be sure of getting through the following weeks was to keep her mind on things outside what she was actually doing.

She was just about to leave her room when the phone rang. Thinking it must be Reception, she lifted the receiver impatiently, and was startled when Denis Cranford answered.

'I've waited all morning to hear from you!' he exclaimed angrily. 'I've had to ask to be put through to you, something I didn't want to do, but it was necessary to discover where you were.'

Paula remembered she had promised to get in touch with him as soon as the others had left. She had forgotten—but then she had had a lot on her mind. Denis shouldn't expect perfect co-operation overnight! Ignoring the lengthy lecture he read her, she said coolly, when he finished, 'Everything went according to plan.'

'Be careful!' he muttered tersely. 'Didn't I warn you not to make remarks like that over the phone?'

Paula grimaced at it, wishing he could see. He was taking everything so seriously while she wasn't able to. At least she hadn't been able to until now. Suddenly her former bravado faded and she was forced to swallow a slight sickness in her throat. Up until now, fooling Luke Armstrong had merely been an idea to play with. But as the time to put the Cranford plan into action was almost upon her, she wasn't finding it so amusing any more.

'How do I get in touch with you, if I'm not here?' she asked, wording her question carefully as she remembered what Denis had said.

'You don't,' he snapped. 'Unless it's imperative, we don't want to hear anything until you have the right news. Then you can leave the rest to us.'

'I'll do my best,' she replied stiffly.

A slight pause, then Denis murmured softly, 'Don't feel deserted, my dear. We'll be thinking of you, and I'm sure you have nothing to worry about.'

Paula felt very angry as she locked her bedroom door and stepped into the lift. Was it her fault that she was driven to consort with creeps like Denis Cranford! If her parents had shown more consideration for her, none of this need have happened. It was partly Ian's fault as well. Hadn't he cast her off as if she was of no more account than a piece of cheap furniture he didn't like? It wasn't because she might have to hurt one of his fellow men that she objected to doing this job; it was the knowledge that she had no alternative but to do it. Not if she wanted to continue living in the style to which she was accustomed!

Luke arrived just before dinner. Paula had began to think he wasn't coming when she glanced up and saw him approaching. This evening, he was wearing a dark dinner jacket and tie, and her heart gave a funny little lurch as she watched him walking towards her. She had to admit he was handsome in a hard sort of way. His thick black hair gleamed with health, while his cool grey eyes and strongly chiselled nose and chin gave him a compelling arrogance. He was tall, well over six foot, and she noticed that the formality of his dress did nothing to disguise his powerful body and limbs.

She had decided to wait for him in a quiet corner of one of the bars, pretending to have a drink. She didn't like being in a bar on her own, but she had known it would be the first place he would search for her.

'Luke!' she exclaimed, in a voice that held relief. 'Am I glad to see you!'

Returning her smile, he sat down beside her, clicking his fingers at a waiter as he did so. He didn't seem to notice she had expressed more than normal pleasure at the sight of him. 'Good evening, Paula,' he grinned, 'I see you're sticking to orange juice.'

'You know what happens,' she reminded him, 'when I try anything stronger.'

'Was it only the drink?' he queried ruefully.

'Will we ever know?' she tossed back.

Luke ordered Bourbon for himself. As the man left to fetch it, he turned to Paula. 'Perhaps I can order for the others, if you can tell me what they'd like. Aren't they down yet?'

'They've—gone,' she replied, speaking hesitantly.

'Gone—where?' he frowned.

'Home,' she said huskily, holding her breath, aware that the next moments might be crucial. She didn't have to try and go pale for effect. She was pale already.

Luke was clearly startled. He accepted his drink from the waiter, but when the man enquired if he wanted anything more, he waved him away.

'Just a minute,' he rasped, staring at Paula intently. 'Let's get this straight. Your workmates have gone back to London, leaving you here alone?' When she nodded numbly, he asked bluntly, 'How come?'

'It wasn't quite like that,' she explained, clasping her hands tightly, doing her best to appear confused. 'I— well, I suppose I may as well tell you. I had a row with Ron at the airport and felt I couldn't sit on the same plane with him, so I decided to come back here for a few more days.'

When Luke spoke, his voice was deep and strained. 'Why didn't you tell me you were leaving, Paula? You promised you would.'

'Because no one told me,' she lied. 'Mrs Hartley did, but not until this morning, and I decided I didn't know you well enough to send you an urgent S.O.S. I was going to write from London,' she assured him hastily, as his mouth went grim.

'The sort of arrived safely, nice meeting you, kind of thing?'

Paula flinched at the irony in his voice. 'Luke,' she retorted indignantly, 'you shouldn't complain. It was because of you that I found the courage to defy Ron, in the first place. He turned—well, really nasty. After the plane had gone, I realised I might have felt forced to go with him, if you hadn't been here to come back to.'

Some of Luke's quick anger seemed to leave him as he took a deep swallow of his whisky. Replacing his glass on the table, he smiled wryly. 'Well, it could have saved me a trip to the U.K.'

Slightly stunned, Paula grasped her orange juice, wishing now that it had been something stronger. Luke might just be talking idly, but somehow she didn't think so. Letting a wistful uncertainty show in her eyes, she smiled at him. 'I really will let you know the next time I'm going home.'

His grey eyes locked with hers and he didn't reply, just went on staring, setting her raw nerves on edge. When at last he broke the silence, she could tell he had been thinking and was trying to be both practical and tactful.

'Can you afford to stay in a place like this, Paula? I realise how, during a quarrel, it's easy to make impulsive decisions.'

'I'm not that impulsive,' she returned dryly, 'nor am I that broke. I've booked for another week, paid in advance. I may have squandered all my hard-earned savings, but they didn't amount to that much, anyway.'

Luke continued watching her closely, as though it was important that he heard every word she said. 'I could offer to help out, but I know your pride wouldn't allow it. What I can do, though,' he paused and smiled at her eagerly, 'is to invite you to stay on the island. I did once before, remember?'

Was she likely to forget! 'When you didn't mention it again,' she said slowly, 'I didn't think you were serious.'

'I didn't mention it again,' he explained ruefully,

'because I didn't want you to feel you were being rushed. I imagined you would feel crowded enough from the attention I was paying you.'

'Oh, Luke!' she faltered charmingly.

'So, how about it?' he asked. 'Will you be my guest?'

Deliberately, she hesitated, conjuring up the tiniest frown. 'I'm not sure that islands are quite my thing . . .'

He gazed at her steadily, never once removing his eyes from the fluctuating colour in her face. 'Why not come and find out? I'm sure you would enjoy the experience. And if it's being alone there with me that's worrying you, I can assure you there's no need. Rose will look after you, she's quite a martinet. She can certainly keep me in my place.'

'It's not just that,' Paula felt herself flushing quite naturally as she bit her lip uncertainly. 'You're very good to me, Luke, and I do appreciate it, but may I have a little time to think it over?'

She suspected he was disappointed, but he immediately agreed. 'Take as long as you like,' he smiled magnanimously. 'At least until after dinner.'

'Bully!' she teased, 'I didn't know you were staying?'

'Try and get rid of me,' he exclaimed mockingly.

It was hard for Paula to find any appetite for her dinner, for the events of the day had taken their toll of her body as well as her mind. Finally she gave up trying to eat and pushed her plate aside.

'Not hungry?' questioned Luke, pursuing his own meal with enjoyment.

'I don't seem to be,' she admitted with a sigh.

He reached out a hand to cover hers as it lay on the table. 'Can you wonder?' he asked grimly. 'I wish I'd been at the airport this morning. It would have given me enormous pleasure to have knocked Davis's teeth in. What was your quarrel about, by the way? You never told me.'

Paula's mind was a jumble of confusion. She had hoped he wouldn't ask. 'I'd rather not talk about it,' she replied reluctantly. 'It wasn't anything important, just one thing leading to another. Then, when I refused to get on the same plane with him, he accused me of staying behind on purpose, to see you, and began using threats.'

'He's in love with you.'

'No,' cynically, Paula shook her head, 'Ron doesn't fall in love. He has affairs, and he hates being thwarted.'

Luke's mouth twisted with a quirk of grim humour. 'Like a lot of men, he doesn't appreciate a woman saying no to him.'

That Luke was lapping it up made her feel more confident. She managed a brave little shrug of her shoulders. 'Ron will soon forget—until I return, anyway.'

Luke frowned darkly. 'Do you have to work with him?'

'Not very much,' she replied lightly, pretending she was more interested in the way he was gently massaging her hand.

As they left the restaurant, Luke suggested that they might look in on the cabaret show in the main restaurant. 'It might help you to relax,' he said. 'I hear the singer is new and very good.'

'You're very well informed,' she teased, 'considering you're not actually staying here.'

'The manager is a cousin of mine,' Luke smiled. 'I believe he gets worried that I might die of loneliness on my island and is always thinking of ways to entice me back to civilisation.'

So that was how he knew the manager! Paula felt a shiver of uneasiness. 'Doesn't he think you're capable of looking after your own interests?' she asked.

Luke laughed at the dryness of her voice. 'He's the kind who never gives up.'

She glanced at him, her eyes sparkling, remembering she was supposed to be trying to captivate him. 'It must be a family trait.'

His white teeth gleamed, but before he could reply a

woman hailed him as they were passing over the foyer. 'Luke, darling!'

As he swung around, Paula saw an exceedingly beautiful woman hurrying towards them. When she caught them up, she threw her arms about Luke's neck and kissed him passionately on the mouth. 'I was hoping I'd find you here this evening, darling,' she exclaimed. 'You haven't been to Bridgetown lately, and I've missed you.'

'Have you?' he smiled, returning her kiss.

Paula, watching the embrace, wondered where her sense of detachment had gone. It puzzled her that she experienced a primitive desire to tear Luke and the dark-haired beauty clinging to him apart. She had never felt like this with Ian, no matter how much he had flirted with other females.

Gently Luke disengaged himself, but he kept hold of the woman's hand as he introduced her to Paula. The two girls acknowledged each other cautiously. Monica Frank stared at Paula coldly, then ignored her.

Her eyes warmed as she concentrated her attention on Luke. 'If you're going to watch the cabaret, darling, would you mind if I joined you? The friends I'm with aren't keen.'

'We'd be delighted,' Luke replied cordially, infuriating Paula by not consulting her. If women like Monica Frank had the nerve to intrude where they weren't wanted, surely he could have found the courage to say no! Unless he didn't want to? He was regarding Monica as if he could be fond of her. Such a thought made Paula feel suddenly apprehensive.

Monica Frank was over thirty and clearly had a mind of her own. She knew what she wanted, and she wanted Luke—it didn't take a genius to work that out. Whether Luke had had an affair with her or not, Paula had no means of knowing, but clearly he had given her some encouragement.

It was at this stage that Paula reminded herself that she didn't own him, and, in a way, it might not be such a bad thing if Monica joined them. It would give her a chance to decide about going to Luke's island. It occurred to her that she might be able to work just as well and far more comfortably—and safely, from the hotel?

During the show, which they viewed from a table reserved for them, Paula cast surreptitious glances at Monica out of the corner of her eye. She was satisfied that her own blue chiffon dress was every bit as smart as the one the other woman was wearing, but she had to admire Monica's diamond necklace and wondered waspishly if it had been a present from Luke. She found herself speculating so much about him and Monica that she suddenly realised that she was completely neglecting far more important problems.

'Enjoying yourself?' Luke's voice in her ear startled her. She had been so deep in thought, she hadn't noticed him leaning towards her.

She gulped and glanced at the glamorous singer whose performance couldn't be faulted. 'Yes,' she nodded.

Luke gazed at her closely. 'The show's good, but I don't think it's getting your full attention.' Keeping his voice low, he added, 'I hope you aren't worrying over my invitation? I told you I'd give you time.'

As he turned to the cabaret again, Paula came to some rapid conclusions. It had been tempting to think she could remain at the hotel, but if she didn't go to Luke's island and her mission failed then the Cranfords might argue that she hadn't tried and they would withhold any kind of reimbursement. Whereas, if she stayed with Luke, whatever the outcome, they couldn't say this. She decided she would spend tonight at the hotel and go to Luke's island in the morning.

She informed him of her decision when the show was over, after Monica had left them. The other girl hadn't been able to find another excuse for neglecting her friends any longer. Luke didn't give any explanation about Monica, but then, Paula pondered, he hadn't told her about the manager of the hotel being his cousin, either. Not until this evening. A man like Luke was bound to know a lot of women. It wouldn't do to worry over them unduly.

Luke appeared delighted that she had at last decided to accept his invitation, and didn't insist that she left with him immediately, instead of in the morning.

'I'll pick you up at ten,' he smiled. 'Leave the cancellation of your room to me.'

'Ten?' Paula protested. 'Isn't that rather early?'

He laughed at her dismayed expression. 'For me that's late.'

'I like my sleep,' she retorted mutinously.

'On the island,' he teased, kissing her lightly as he left her, 'if we can't change your bad habits, you can sleep as long as you like.'

Paula discovered that to be ready at ten she had to be up before nine. There were clothes to repack and, perhaps because she hadn't a lot, she liked to pack carefully. Then she had to shower and dress and make sure she hadn't left anything behind.

When the boutique in the hotel opened she purchased two pairs of lightweight pants in a serviceable, easy-to-wash cotton. She resisted everything else but a black leotard which she considered she might need to keep her weight down. In the country, at home, she had always loved jogging, if only for the sense of freedom it gave. Plenty of people jogged in London, of course, but she never felt like it in town.

Next she paid a visit to the hotel bookshop where she selected several paperbacks by her favourite authors. Books were what she hated having to economise on most. All her life she had been used to buying them by the armful. Luke might have some on his island, but even if he happened to be literarily minded, it was unlikely they shared the same tastes. She loved books so much, she had once thought of trying to write one herself but had never got further than thinking about it.

She packed her books out of sight in the bottom of a

bag. If Luke didn't read much—and many men never read much more than the daily paper, it might put him off to discover she was a bit of a bookworm. The best she could hope for was that he was fond of music. Somehow, from the way he had responded to the beat of it while they had danced, she felt music might be in his blood. It would be nice if he had a few of her favourite records and the means to play them on his island. At least it might help to pass the time.

Luke arrived while she was having breakfast in one of the restaurants. 'Any coffee going spare?' he asked, sinking his large frame in the chair opposite.

'Sure, plenty.' A waiter, following him, brought him a cup and Paula pushed the coffee pot towards him.

'Still feeling lazy this morning, are you?' he mocked, helping himself.

'Umm,' she buttered a croissant with extra care in order to keep her eyes off him. Why did he always have to look so super? she wondered dismally. It would have been much simpler if he'd been plain and uninteresting, so she wouldn't have felt attracted to him. Even in jeans and a white body shirt with his dark hair rumpled, he managed to have a peculiar effect on her.

'I've seen Peter about your room,' he told her, as he stirred sugar into his coffee. 'He's keeping it for you, for fear, as I recall you put it, the island isn't your thing. You can collect your days here, whenever you like. Or have a refund.'

His cousin, Peter Gerrard, was there as they were leaving. Paula had seen him several times, but that was all. She had made a point of keeping her distance from the hotel staff, so as not to arouse any unnecessary curiosity.

Peter Gerrard was a man in his forties and very pleasant. He didn't seem nearly as aggressive as Luke. She was gratified, though, to see the same admiration in his eyes as they stood chatting in the morning sunshine and he studied her delicate young beauty.

'I hear you're going to visit Devil's Island,' he smiled.

'What did you say?' she gasped.

Luke threw his cousin an exasperated glance as Paula went pale. 'That's just Peter's idea of a joke,' he sighed. 'He's been there once when the weather broke, but it was his own fault. He knew rough weather was forecast.'

Peter laughed. 'I always swear Luke conjured up that storm on purpose, to get rid of me. He doesn't like people disturbing his peace. Of course, you can understand why, Miss Edison.'

'Call her Paula,' Luke intervened abruptly. 'And we really have to go, Pete.'

His cousin glanced at him thoughtfully but didn't argue. 'Goodbye, then, Paula,' he held out his hand. 'I expect Luke will be bringing you over for dinner, one evening, when you tire of all that splendid isolation?'

This morning, Luke's boat was moored by the hotel jetty instead of further along the coast. The sun was already hot as they cast off but Paula didn't mind. She still felt cold from the chill that had struck her when Peter had referred to Luke's home as Devil's Island. While she was sensible enough to recognise a joke when she heard one, she couldn't get rid of the feeling that if Peter's trip had been unfortunate, hers might easily be a downright disaster!

Trying to get rid of the depression that plagued her, she went to stand beside Luke as he skilfully manoeuvred his boat around some much larger yachts and made for the open seas. She watched his hands on the tiller. They were large but well shaped and strong. Again she wondered what he did.

As if able to read her thoughts and seeking to divert them, he spoke first. 'You can't have seen much of Barbados yet. I shouldn't have dragged you away.'

'I've been here before,' she said carelessly. 'A long time ago,' she added quickly. 'I was only a child—my parents brought me. We stayed at the Hilton, or somewhere like that.'

Luke said dryly, 'Your parents obviously liked the best.'

'They preferred Jamaica,' she shrugged. 'They travelled a lot. All islands began to seem much the same to me.'

'You're older now, though.'

'Yes,' she conceded, lifting her face to the wind, knowing what he was driving at, 'I suppose I could always take another look at Barbados when I come back?'

'Maybe I can show it to you?' he laughed, drawing her suddenly close to hug her. 'I like your pants,' he remarked, just as quickly releasing her and lightly slapping her bottom. 'I thought you said you hadn't any?'

'I hadn't!' she retorted indignantly, rubbing both hands over curves that tingled disturbingly. 'I found them this morning in the hotel boutique. So there's no need to punish me,' she reproved unthinkingly, 'for trying to deceive you.'

'My apologies,' he grinned. 'I didn't mean to hurt your—er—feelings. Perhaps I should kiss you better?' Catching her to him again, he proceeded to do so, so thoroughly that by the time he finished she was accusing him of taking all her breath.

'I can't do a thing right, can I?' he complained.

Paula found herself giggling at the righteous hurt he displayed. Laughing with Luke was becoming an addiction; perhaps she should watch out. It must be much easier to make a fool of someone one disliked? And when she talked to Luke and he kissed her, she wasn't sure it was dislike she felt.

Because such thoughts made her apprehensive, she offered to make some coffee, an offer Luke quickly accepted.

'I see you're going to be very useful,' he chuckled. 'I think I might take you sailing for a few days. I can fish while you do the work.'

'What you want is a galley-slave,' she retorted wryly as she went below. She hoped he would forget about fishing trips. It dismayed her that dangerous new aspects of the situation she had got herself into were arising all the time. Living on the island with Luke would be bad enough, but his servants would be there. She couldn't bear to think of the additional intimacy a fishing trip conjured up.

Henry was waiting when they reached Sabina, which Luke had disclosed over coffee was the real name of his island. He had denied having called it after a girl-friend. It had already been named when he purchased it, but he had said he would tell her about that another day.

Henry carried Paula's luggage to the house while Luke brought some stores from the boat that had been ordered by Rose. 'She said that several things were needed if I had a woman coming to stay,' he grinned.

Paula glanced at him doubtfully, her cheeks slightly pink. 'I don't want to make a lot of extra work. I'm sure your servants have enough to do.'

'Call them Rose and Henry,' he muttered, glancing at Henry's broad back on the path in front of them. 'We don't stand on ceremony here, and I'm sure you'll be the perfect guest.'

Paula replied meekly that she'd try to be, and was rewarded by a warm smile. She hoped Luke wouldn't expect her to get too friendly with Rose. The well-worn concept she was familiar with in books of the heroine and housekeeper becoming bosom pals didn't impress her. Besides, she was the villainess of the piece, wasn't she? Rose might thank her for not being too friendly when one day she discovered how Paula had deceived her beloved master!

They continued on the path silently. The trade winds which kept some of the heat at bay at sea didn't seem to penetrate the thick jungle foliage around them, and Paula was hot and exhausted by the time they reached the house. When Luke asked Rose to fetch her a cool drink, she glanced at him gratefully.

The bedroom Luke showed her to was spacious but, like the rest of the house, sparsely furnished. Apart from the bed, there was only a wardrobe and a large

chest with a mirror perched on top. The bed was wide
but looked hard, the only concession to comfort the
small rug by the side of it. The rest of the floor was
bare.

Paula frowned doubtfully at the floor. 'Doesn't it
collect the dust?' she asked.

'Rose mops through every day,' Luke replied.
'Carpets would be too hot.'

But much to be preferred, Paula thought, shuddering
to imagine her feet on such bare boards in the cool of
the night. Moodily she turned her gaze to Luke. His
large body seemed to fill the whole doorway as he
lounged indolently against the frame. His left leg was set
at an angle that stretched the material of his blue jeans
tautly across his muscular thighs. Paula blinked as one
of the unrecognisable sensations she had experienced in
his company lately rushed through her, and she
quickly averted her eyes.

As his glance skimmed slowly over her slender, well
proportioned body, she wondered apprehensively what
was on his mind. In some ways Luke was an enigma.
How was she to get through the next few weeks with a
man like him? The task before her seemed suddenly
monumental. Was it possible to reduce someone who
she suspected still retained some of the basic instincts of
his more primitive ancestors to a puppet ready to obey
her slightest whim?

'I want you to make yourself at home,' Luke
advanced to where she was standing regarding both him
and her surroundings uncertainly. 'If you don't like
your room, it's an easy matter to change it.'

'It's quite adequate, thank you.' She didn't suppose
the others were very different.

'My room is just along the passage,' he informed her
softly.

When she frowned at him, unconsciously wary, he
reached out to draw her against his hard, warm chest.
Her mind cried in protest at his nearness. Why must he
always be taking hold of her?

He tenderly kissed her temple, a dark golden eyebrow and the tip of her nose, then softly captured her lips in a kiss that was far more devastating than his passionate kisses of earlier in the morning. Without being aware of what she was doing, Paula slipped her arms around his waist, pulling him tightly to her. She could feel his breath on her neck as she buried her hot face against him. Her slender body seemed to fit perfectly into the taller proportions of his, the top of her silken head just reaching his shoulder. Sighing gently, she found herself doing something she had never done before. Turning her mouth, she kissed the base of his strong throat as they stood holding each other closely.

She hadn't reckoned on the effect this would have on him. She actually felt him tremble. 'My God, Paula, you're beautiful!' he muttered huskily in her ear, his tongue circling its shell-like perfection.

Immediately his lips touched her ear, shivers of awareness and fright washed along Paula's spine. What on earth was she doing letting herself respond to him like this? Fear cooled her face as she pushed him away, although, when she saw him staring at her narrowly, she forced herself to smile.

'Like whisky in the morning, it's too early,' she mumbled, in a kind of confused attempt to explain her sudden rejection of him.

His mouth quirked with immediate amusement. 'It would never be too early for me.'

She gulped, unable to reply in the same vein. 'D-do Henry and Rose sleep in the house?' she stammered awkwardly.

'Oh, Paula,' he sighed, 'you're so transparent! You should know by this time that you have nothing to fear. I would never make love to you without your consent, and anyway, we haven't got that far yet. As for Rose and Henry, their quarters are at the back of the house, but I'm sure you won't be needing their protection.'

Paula wasn't so sure, but she merely swallowed and

said, 'I think I'll rest before lunch. You could send Rose to do my unpacking.'

Luke gave her a sharp glance which she didn't see. 'Yes,' he shrugged, 'I expect you're tired.'

When he had left her, Paula found the bathroom and took a shower. Though there was plenty of hot water, the plumbing looked positively ancient. The bath was huge but stood on legs, one of which was rusty. She wished she'd had a bathroom adjoining her own room. This arrangement wasn't very convenient, but she supposed she would just have to put up with it.

Rose came in as she was resting, to do her unpacking. She was inclined to chatter, but Paula paid her little attention, so Rose finally gave up talking to herself and with a puzzled glance at the girl lying on the bed, returned to her preparations for lunch.

Paula spent the remainder of the day reading and generally lazing about. When Luke tried to persuade her to go for a walk with him she yawned and refused. As an excuse, she pretended she had a headache which she wanted to get rid of before dinner.

'Dinner's hours away,' he frowned. 'A walk beside the sea and some fresh air might clear your head and give you an appetite.'

'That's one thing I can do without,' she retorted stubbornly, staying where she was.

She took exactly two hours getting ready for dinner, going through the ritual of washing and setting her hair, varnishing her nails and making her face up elaborately. She was disappointed to find, on reaching the lounge, after taking so much trouble over her own appearance, that Luke had done nothing more than change into another pair of slacks and a clean shirt.

Wondering if he was going to accuse her of being overdressed, she felt slightly relieved when the hard impatience died from his face as he bent to kiss her.

Regarding her shining gold and red beauty, her exclusive harem trousers and camisole top, he shook his head ruefully. 'You put me to shame!'

Paula smiled graciously and let him kiss her again, but this time, when he would have deepened the kiss, she reminded him sharply of her immaculate make-up. 'You've no idea how long it takes to do properly, Luke,' she protested. 'I don't want it finishing up all over your shirt!'

'I like you better without it,' he muttered, ignoring her horrified look.

The dinner Rose served was delicious. Paula agreed that Rose was a wonderful cook, but she saw no reason for Luke to congratulate her so warmly. After all, that was what servants were for. They were paid to be efficient, weren't they?

'Could you run my bath about ten, Rose, please?' she requested coolly, when the woman brought in their coffee. To Luke she spoke equally distantly. 'I think I'll have an early night.'

It wasn't until Rose had gone that she felt a distinct chill in the air and realised something was wrong. The atmosphere was so thick with Luke's disapproval, she could have cut it with a knife. Oh, God! she groaned inwardly, despairing of her own stupidity as it suddenly dawned on her what it was. Couldn't she get anything right? Was she doomed to make a mess of her life! For the past few hours she had dwelt in cloud-cuckoo-land, thinking how lovely it was to have servants again and pretending the old days were back. Perhaps Luke was right when he'd said she was mixed up! And it wasn't as if she'd enjoyed having servants all that much—how often had she scorned her mother for relying on them completely?

Luke had noticed her ordering Rose about. He was annoyed, and who could blame him? The motherly Bajon had probably been his nursemaid or something, while Paula Edison was a girl he had only known a few days. With angry dismay, Paula became aware that she might easily have undone all the hard work she had put in over the past week. She had managed to attract Luke's attention and learned to endure his unwelcome embraces, yet, through her own lack of foresight, it might all come to nothing.

Stealing a glance at his grim face, she decided against offering immediate apologies which, she sensed might be somewhat in the nature of waving a red flag in the front of a bull. It might be better to wait until tomorrow and give him a chance to cool down, then she would apologise to Rose. Somehow she must convince Luk she wasn't the spoiled creature he thought her to be. She refused to listen to the shameful doubt that assailed her, that if he did think this he might be right. In the morning she must do her best to convince him that she had been tired and overwrought, and still on edge because of her quarrel with Ron Davis. If she managed to do this humbly enough, with just the right degree of tearful remorse, surely he would forgive her, and then everything would be all right again.

# CHAPTER FIVE

WHEN Paula woke the next morning she discovered she had overslept, which was unfortunate as she had been determined to make a good impression by rising at the crack of dawn. If Luke did nothing all day but laze around, he might not be up, either, but she suspected he was an early riser. Hadn't he said he was? Consoling herself that she couldn't be expected to correct all her bad habits immediately, she rolled out of bed with a groan. The bed had proved to be as hard as it looked; it had been ages before she had fallen asleep. She hoped the Cranfords appreciated the tribulations she was having to suffer in order to earn the money they were paying her.

After a quick shower she hastily pulled on a pair of pants and a silky shirt and went to see if she could find anyone. Luke wasn't around, but Rose was.

'You want breakfast, Miss Edison?' Rose asked politely.

'Thank you, Rose, and the name's Paula.' Paula forced an anxious expression to her face as she said contritely, 'I'm sorry if I put you to a lot of trouble yesterday, Rose. I'm sure you've enough to do without running after me, but, what with one thing and another, I seem to have had a terrible week, and yesterday I wasn't myself.'

Rose's dark brown eyes softened warmly at such an abject apology. 'Think nothing of it, Miss Paula,' she said.

'I really am very sorry,' Paula stressed.

Rose shook her head, and the beaming smile on her face assured Paula she had made a friend for life.

'If there's anything at all I can do to help, Rose,' she offered sweetly, 'you have only to ask.'

She was relieved when Rose replied that there wasn't. With another wide smile, she said she was used to managing by herself.

'Has Luke had breakfast yet?' Paula enquired nervously.

'Yes, hours ago.' Rose sounded amused. 'Soon, though, if I know him, he'll be here looking for coffee.'

She didn't say where he was, but he could only be somewhere on the island. Probably out for a walk? Paula had just finished her breakfast when he appeared.

'Hello,' he greeted her briefly. 'How are you this morning?'

He sounded friendly enough, but as she glanced at him quickly, Paula saw that his eyes were still wary. She was thankful she had come to her senses in time. 'I'm feeling much better, thank you,' she let her voice quiver slightly. 'My black mood seems to have gone.'

'Ah . . .' On his way to the other end of the table, Luke paused then returned to her. His eyes fixed on her face, he drew her gently to her feet. Last night he had left her almost immediately after dinner, to deal with some mail in his study, and she hadn't seen him again. She knew she was getting another chance and must make the most of it.

'Yesterday,' he said carefully, 'you changed . . .'

Paula swallowed pathetically. 'Yesterday things suddenly seemed to become too much for me. I nearly asked you to take me back to the mainland so I could go home. I don't know why I felt so wretched?'

'Oh, sweetheart!' Luke pressed his mouth against her cheek as he held her lightly, before kissing her trembling lips. 'We all react differently to stress. I should have guessed. In my arrogance, I began wondering if I'd made a mistake about you.'

Tears filled Paula's eyes, tears that startled her because she hadn't been trying to produce any. Irrationally she was tempted to bury her head against Luke's broad shoulder and weep, letting months of accumulative misery wash out. With an effort she pulled herself together. Why be so miserable when there was nothing wrong with her life? Luke wasn't angry and she refused to look further than the present. Everything would be all right, once she had lulled his suspicions.

As he kissed her tenderly, she smiled at him through the tears which, unwittingly, made her seem very young and vulnerable. 'I'm sorry,' she whispered, 'I didn't mean to weep all over you.'

'That's my girl,' he murmured huskily, appraising her apparent courage with something warm in his eyes that shook her slightly as he lifted her chin to plant another loving kiss on her mouth. 'Let's forget yesterday, shall we? It's a beautiful morning, why don't we go down to the sea and have a swim?'

'Oh, that would be lovely!' she gulped, agreeing radiantly, feeling she would have jumped over a cliff, had he suggested it.

'Go and find something suitable to wear, then, while I grab some coffee,' he grinned, releasing her with a gentle push. 'I daren't suggest we swim with nothing on, as I do, when I'm alone.'

'Th-that's what you'd been doing when we first met,' she stammered, suddenly remembering.

'Yes,' he regarded her pink cheeks with amusement. 'There's nothing quite like it.'

'Well, I don't intend finding out,' she retorted primly, escaping to her room, followed by his taunting laughter.

Quickly she changed into a one-piece swimsuit. Luke had liked her in the bikinis he had seen her in previously, but she wanted to impress him in a different way. She sensed she would have to make him love her, not just lust after her, if she were to stand a chance of persuading him to leave his island.

Returning to the dining-room, she began gathering up their dishes and was loading them on a tray when Luke asked sharply what she was doing.

'I'm trying to help Rose,' she explained, smiling at him ruefully. 'I guess I took my frustration out on her as well as you, yesterday, and I'd like to make amends. I've already apologised, but there's nothing like concrete evidence to really prove I'm sorry, is there?'

Firmly he took the tray from her and set it aside. 'Rose will understand, honey. And she won't appreciate you helping her any more than she did your ordering her about. Like most women, she's contrary. Perhaps if you just stick to making your bed, huh? A little gesture like that, which she can pretend not to see, will keep her happy. She won't think you're poaching on her preserves.'

'You should have been a P.R. man,' Paula teased, 'or is it just women you understand so well?'

On the way to the beach, she asked, 'How long have Rose and Henry been with you, Luke?'

'A long time,' he replied idly. 'Henry probably saved my life one night in New York and when I discovered he had no permanent employment, I asked him and his wife if they'd like to come here and look after me. They've been with me ever since.'

Luke wasn't being very explicit, but Paula merely asked. 'Aren't they lonely on the island?'

'They don't complain,' Luke answered briefly. 'They have plenty of friends on Barbados whom they visit regularly. They spent a couple of days there last week.'

Paula glanced at him quickly as he strolled by her side. He wasn't telling her much, but maybe there wasn't much to tell. Yet, with the extra sensitivity she was developing towards him, she knew he was holding a lot back. There was information regarding both himself and his servants that, for some reason, he withheld. Ah, well, she thought philosophically, it couldn't be anything important.

The water was warm and buoyant; Paula couldn't remember when she'd enjoyed swimming so much. She was good in the water, swimming naturally, with a lot of grace. Luke swam well, too, though far more powerfully than she did. It was his strength and ability to manoeuvre that enabled him to frequently catch hold of her and plant warm kisses on her protesting mouth. Eventually, when she grew tired of refusing him and gave in, she began to find pleasure in their kisses and sensuously entangled limbs. If she hadn't been involved in such a dangerous game with the Cranfords she might have been able to relax completely. As it was, her commitment to them was always there at the back of her mind.

The following days passed slowly. Paula blamed the isolation and loneliness of the island for the unsettling effect it had on her, and, as an antidote, she read more and slept a lot. Sometimes, when Luke wasn't around, she got Henry to carry a lounger into the overgrown garden for her and lazed for hours in the sun. Neither Henry nor Luke seemed inclined to make a start on the garden, though Luke declared it should be done.

Occasionally, when Luke disappeared into his study in the more distant regions of the house, she tried to explore the island. He had shown her some of it and she didn't discover much more by herself, but once, she found a hidden track leading to a high summit, from which she was able to judge the potential of Sabina and to understand why the Cranfords were so eager to have it. About four miles in circumference, with spectacular terrain and views, properly developed, the island could be a veritable goldmine. Paula sat and stared about her, that day, for a long time. What a fool she had been to imagine what the Cranfords had offered to pay her was more than generous! They would have to sink a lot of money in Sabina, of course, but they might eventually reap millions.

Paula didn't exactly remember when the whole idea of a hotel here became repugnant to her. And when it did, she didn't understand it. Long before anything was built she would be gone. Besides, developers like the Cranfords enhanced, they didn't destroy. They would tame it, though, a small voice whispered; all the splendid wildness would disappear. It would become just another place the idle rich would patronize for amusement.

Uneasy with such thoughts, Paula didn't encourage them. She began restricting herself to wandering by the sea or staying in the garden. Dimly she realised her growing interest in the island must be ignored. Soon she would be gone, never to return.

When Luke found her reading a book one evening, she felt puzzled that he obviously didn't believe she really liked them. So far, during the two weeks of her visit, he had spent almost every evening with her, but tonight, after dinner, he had said he was expecting a call and had gone to wait for it in his study. Paula had fetched a book from her room, thinking it would be a good opportunity to find out who had committed the murder in her latest whodunit, but she hadn't been able to concentrate. She had had other things on her mind—chiefly Luke, and somehow the book had got twisted upside down, an anomaly Luke had immediately noticed when he had unexpectedly returned and lifted the book from her hands.

His brows rose as he closed it and studied the name splashed in gold letters across the blue cover. 'I don't remember buying this.'

'You didn't,' Paula shrugged. 'I picked it up in the hotel.'

'A favourite author of yours?'

Again she was wary of letting him think she was bookish for fear it didn't go with the image she was trying to create. 'He's all right,' she replied indifferently.

Luke's mouth twisted. 'Why pretend you like reading if you don't?'

. She was startled. She had made a better job of impressing him than she'd intended. She couldn't understand though, why he should look so suspicious. 'I wasn't pretending . . .' she faltered.

'Paula!' his grey eyes glinted with sudden impatience, 'I want no more pretence between us.'

She didn't follow and thought he was referring to something else. 'What are you talking about?' she whispered, her green eyes widening with fright.

'Nothing to alarm you to that extent,' he retorted dryly, sitting down beside her. 'I just want you to be yourself. More importantly, I want you to stop going tense every time I come near you.'

'You're wrong,' she exclaimed, dismayed that he had sensed things about her that she had thought well concealed.

'Come here,' he admonished. 'Let me show you.'

She flinched as he took her in his arms and felt his lips lie for a moment against the top of her head as he waited for her to relax. Then he turned her face up so he could look at her. Their eyes met and locked for an interminable time. 'See?' Luke murmured.

Paula felt her heart suddenly pounding against her ribs as she nodded helplessly. It was fright, she was being threatened, she told herself weakly. It was always the same, yet, with Luke, along with the icy stiffening there was also a strange heat. This new sensation was something she still didn't understand. Could it mean that, underneath, she wasn't the frozen icicle she had always thought herself to be?

She was wearing a strappy silk dress, little more than a scrap of material. Luke brushed a hand along one of her bare arms, making her skin burn with awareness. 'I can't keep my hands off you,' he said roughly. 'Can't you feel the electricity between us?'

Her breath caught in her throat as she tried to move away, but he refused to allow it. Instead, he pulled her closer to him so that she felt the hard virility of his body pressing against her as his lips feathered light kisses on her face.

'Please, Luke!' she squirmed. 'What if Rose should find us?'

'They've retired hours ago and you know she doesn't come back until morning.'

'We can't be certain . . .' she began, but he silenced her protests with a hard demanding kiss, this time on her mouth, not her cheek. She felt her lips forced apart as his began a darting exploration.

Against her will a kind of excitement was growing inside her, and her hands which had started to push him away were suddenly clinging to him. After satiating himself of her mouth, he slid the straps of her dress from her shoulders so he could press warm kisses on the tender hollows he found there, before moving on to her breasts. Her dress still half covered them and he pushed it impatiently further down so he could have easier access to them. As his hands caressed them, his tongue tantalised the pink nipples until she suddenly found it almost impossible to breathe and wondered desperately what was happening to her.

Dear God! she gasped inwardly, almost overcome by the burning, devouring feeling rapidly consuming her. Even her legs were weakened by it; she wouldn't be able to move, even had she wanted to! Had Luke Armstrong no mercy? She shivered with the awareness of his hard body so close to her own and her mounting, confusing response to it. His fingers moved cunningly, with knowing expertise, while his mouth made no allowance for her innocence. He overwhelmed her, scattering her inhibitions, releasing such a flood of liquid fire into her veins that she thought she was either burning up or drowning.

She had only her voice left to fight him with, and even that was difficult to find. 'Luke, don't ...' she entreated hoarsely.

'Stop resisting me, Paula,' he lifted his head, his eyes smouldering. 'God knows I want you and you want me, so what's the problem? If you go on as you're doing, you'll drive us both insane!'

'I'm not doing anything ...'

'Paula!' he groaned in exasperation, while his mouth continued to torment hers, his tongue outlining her soft lips sensuously.

She had to close her eyes against another invasion of sensations hitherto unknown to her. She found it difficult to think coherently. The madness in her body was clouding her brain—she could only move her head unsteadily from side to side.

She wasn't just shaking her head in denial of what Luke was saying, she was trying to clear it. She had to be able to think to protect herself. Luke posed a potent threat to her carefully laid plans, for he could reduce her to the state of not knowing what she was doing.

'Let me sit up,' she begged, as he pressed her down on the sofa.

He was blind and deaf to her pleading. 'I won't let you escape. You know you want me.'

It was expedient to be honest for once. Luke's insistence frightened her, and against her will she was forced to nod.

Her hot, then paling, cheeks were viewed with mounting derision. 'Why be so coy, darling? Or do you like your men to beg?'

'No . . .' He was groping for her zipper, clearly intent on removing her dress altogether. What was she to do? No clear answer. Frantically she fought the fog she was in, trying to find one.

As Luke had already discovered, she wasn't wearing a bra—a shameful habit she had only acquired since coming to the island. It wasn't one she approved of, but she found it more comfortable to go without. The removal of her dress gave Luke easier access to her breasts, and, as his mouth assaulted them again, her nipples tautened until he muttered triumphantly. 'Your body welcomes me, Paula. Why deny it the satisfaction it obviously craves?'

She knew then that she really had to get away from him. Attempting to put some distance between them, while there might still be time, she pushed her hands against his chest, but only managed to dislodge a button of his shirt. Underneath, the curling hairs on his skin sent astonishing feelings shooting up her arm from her tingling fingers.

'That's better,' he growled, as she drew a sharp breath. Dealing with the rest of the buttons himself, he threw his shirt off and pulled her closer.

Paula shuddered as she was crushed tightly against

the roughness her fingers had been caressing. His hands moved to her closed lids, tracing their contours lightly. Then his mouth was stirring moistly over her cheeks to find her shaking lips in a kiss which was utterly and purely sensational.

As she was subject to the kind of kissing she had never experienced before, there was fear within her but also a bewildering excitement. And, in those moments, there was only herself and Luke, no one else. Rose and Henry were forgotten, along with the Cranfords.

Luke's drugging kisses prevented her from thinking of anyone but him. All resistance fled, her arms going tightly around his neck as his mouth moved insidiously, devilishly conspiring with his hands to drive her mindless. She didn't remember when he picked her up and carried her to her bedroom.

In dazed seconds, she was lying on the bed, slightly shocked but still unable to prevent Luke from doing what he liked with her. Her heart raced madly as she heard his slacks following his belt to the floor before he lay down beside her. Longing shook her slender body as he bent to brush her bare shoulder with his lips while his arms crushed her to his hard length. Funny noises she could hear distinctly but couldn't stop seemed to be issuing from her trembling mouth as she clutched him wildly. She felt him shudder involuntarily, the muscles of his stomach tightening against her as he threw his body over hers, demanding her final surrender.

Pressing down on her with his full weight, his hands slipped into the softness of her hair. 'You're a witch,' he muttered thickly, 'you have some hold over me. I can't escape, but neither can you. I hope you realise that, my darling?'

She couldn't reply. His mouth was branding hers with burning kisses while his right hand shifted from the side of her breast to her thighs. At this precise moment, the one last flicker of sanity left in her brain somehow became strong enough to enable her to gasp incoherently, 'I haven't done this before, Luke!'

Because, in this instance, she was speaking the truth, the sincerity in her voice must have got through to him. At her strangled appeal, the gathering momentum of his body stilled, then jerked, as though he had been dealt a powerful blow. He remained rigid, his breathing laboured, and when Paula managed to look at him, she found him gazing down on her with blazing eyes.

'You're sure?' he asked at last.

'I'm sorry,' she whispered through a tight throat.

'You're a virgin?'

Paula swallowed. His face had a grey cast where before it had been flushed. Her eyes filled with tears from an emotion she couldn't define as she nodded.

'My God!' He didn't immediately leave her but buried his face in a pillow. 'I didn't realise. I know you're young, but I thought . . .'

Paula listened to his groaning self-reproaches with something like disbelief. He sounded quite shattered. She felt pain tearing at her heart but didn't know what it was.

'I've never cared for any man enough to give myself to him,' she felt compelled to try and explain. 'I don't sleep around.'

Luke raised his head, his smouldering glance still reflecting an inferno of desire, but she saw, from the tightness of his mouth, that his feelings were now firmly under control. 'How have you managed not to, I wonder, with a passionate nature like yours?'

Colour crept under Paula's skin as she huddled under the sheet she had grasped in order to hide her bare limbs. She ached all over. She couldn't believe she had a passionate nature though she suddenly felt weak and wild when she recalled how she had felt in his arms. She longed to throw her own arms about him again but she stiffened even as her pulse quickened crazily. She hadn't changed. Luke had taken her by surprise, that was all. If she was like he said she was, how could she have resisted him? No, she was frigid and always had been, but if she tried to convince Luke of this he might only laugh.

'I'm not one of these people who's only interested in sex,' she retorted sharply. 'I'm sorry, Luke, but that's the way I'm made.'

Surprisingly, the terse impatience on Luke's face faded and was replaced by tender warmth. 'Stop worrying, Paula,' he said gently, lifting a gentle hand to caress her hot cheeks. 'I think I've told you before that I don't believe you know what you want, or how you're made, but it's too late to argue about that tonight. You'd better try and get some sleep or Rose will be accusing me of heaven knows what in the morning!' As she stirred restlessly, he dropped a lingering kiss on her mouth before sliding off the bed and leaving her.

Paula watched him go. He didn't look back as her eyes blindly followed his tall, perfectly muscled body until the door closed behind him. Then, burying her face in her hands, she began to weep.

Luke was nowhere to be seen when she went to the dining-room for breakfast. This was nothing new, but, because she had got up early, she had thought he might be around. She looked through one of the French windows that opened out on to the garden, but there was no sign of him there, either. She had taken great pains with her appearance this morning. The brief shorts she was wearing flattered her long, slim legs and she had brushed her red-gold curls until they shone. She wasn't sure why she had gone to so much trouble, unless it was to make up for lost ground. Now she had refused to sleep with him, there was a danger that Luke might have lost interest in her. She hoped not, but it was always a possibility.

'Where's Luke this morning?' she asked, as Rose came in with her coffee, the casual brightness of her smile not exactly reflecting her feelings.

'In his study, Miss Paula. Looks like he bin there half the night.'

'In his study?' Paula frowned. 'What on earth does he do there all the time, Rose?'

'He doesn't talk about it,' Rose replied stolidly.

Rose was clamming up on her, as she usually did, on the subject of Luke's work, and it couldn't be all that important. 'He probably just sleeps,' she said waspishly.

'I have slept there,' came his voice from behind her.

'Oh!' Startled, Paula glanced up at him over her shoulder. 'I think I must change the position of my chair so I'll be able to see you coming.'

His smile was not his usual effortless one. As Rose departed, though, he bent to kiss her lightly on her upturned mouth as he passed her to sit down. 'I didn't sleep last night,' he murmured in her ear.

Averting her eyes, Paula gulped uncertainly. 'I'm sorry. I suppose it was my fault.'

'Not mine,' he quipped dryly.

As she poured his coffee and gave it to him, he met her anxious glance. 'If I seem particularly despondent this morning, my love, it's not entirely your fault. I've just received word that someone on the mainland wants to see me.'

Had he hesitated before saying someone? That he didn't invite her to accompany him increased her suspicions that the message had been from a woman— maybe Monica Frank. She was inclined to reconsider, however, when after another moment he added, with a hint of self-derision, 'I might have taken you with me, but I may get held up, and I don't want you running about on your own and perhaps forsaking me for an American millionaire.'

Paula would have liked to have come, if only to break the monotony of her voluntary exile, but she didn't try to make Luke change his mind. It might not pay to let him think she was becoming too possessive. 'I might be safer here,' she agreed, with a teasing smile.

She walked to the boat with him. The sun was already high in the sky. It promised to be an especially beautiful day. 'We haven't had any visitors since I came,' she remarked idly, by the empty jetty.

Luke caught her to him forcibly, his hands hard on her waist. 'Have you ever wanted anyone but me?'

'Of course not,' she replied, but lowered her lashes for fear he should notice the reservation in her eyes. Making an effort, she sighed heavily. 'Perhaps I'm trying not to let you know how much I'm going to miss you—even for a day.'

With a throaty grunt of satisfaction, he dug his fingers into her flesh, while his mouth brushed further words from her lips. He seemed reluctant to let her go. 'When I get back,' he said huskily, his eyes brilliant, 'we have to talk.'

Smiling wistfully, Paula nodded as he kissed her again before releasing her and jumping lightly on board. She watched his lithe figure moving agilely about the deck as he prepared the boat for sailing. Then suddenly the engine sprang to life and spray swirled as he steered away from where she was standing into the sparkling blue waters of the lagoon.

'Be good,' he grinned with a wave, and she wondered ironically what else she could be. The island was as good as a prison!

The day stretched endlessly. Rose and Henry retired to their own quarters after lunch, and Paula felt haunted by the silence around her. In the noonday heat, even the birds had stopped singing. She couldn't understand the peculiar mood she was in. She knew Luke had something to do with it, and while she was reluctant to recall his passionate lovemaking of the night before, she realised she should be considering at least the implications of it.

It was obvious that Luke was attracted to her. What she had to do now was to deepen his feelings towards her until he either asked her to marry him or offered some kind of permanent relationship which she could accept. Under certain conditions! The most important being that he left Sabina. During the past few days she had tried to pretend a growing aversion to it, so it shouldn't be too difficult to convince him she couldn't live here.

She didn't believe he would deny her anything that

really mattered to her, but there was no harm in going over everything, just to make sure she got it right. After Luke proposed something to her, whether marriage or an affair, and agreed to leave the island, she must get in touch with the Cranfords. She would ask him if she could ring them from here and pretend she was speaking to her agent. It was all arranged. The Cranfords would understand exactly what she meant when she said she was getting married, or whatever, and would require no more modelling work for the time being.

After spending the afternoon sleeping in the garden Paula, as usual, went to a great deal of trouble over dressing for dinner. For all she told herself she wasn't the least bit nervous of Luke Armstrong she knew a great desire to complete the job she had agreed to do for the Cranfords as soon as possible. It was proving both disturbing and embarrassing, she acknowledged with a shudder. Apart from this, she had discovered she had no taste for accepting hospitality from someone she was expected to deceive.

How Luke's kisses had affected her the night before was something else that filled her with an increasing urgency to get away from him. Why she had never experienced the same feelings with Ian as she did with Luke, she didn't know. Hollowly she admitted she might not have been a virgin now if she had. The sooner she was in London and back to her old way of life, the better she would like it!

She could have screamed in despair when, after she had taken so much care over her appearance, Rose came to inform her that Luke had been held up. 'Luke says he's very sorry, Miss Paula, and he'll be home some time tomorrow.'

Paula could scarcely eat her dinner for wondering if it was Monica that was detaining him. The question kept entering her head, worrying her. It seemed unfair that all the effort she had put into charming Luke might be wasted if Monica Frank was back on the scene. What a fool she had been to let him go to Barbados without her! Thinking of him dining with another woman made her feel sick—though, she told herself vehemently, it wasn't with jealousy. If there hadn't been so much at stake, he could have spent the night with half a dozen women, for all she cared!

He didn't return until late the following afternoon, by which time Paula was so relieved to see him that she almost threw her arms around him. She had nearly given him up!

'I've missed you!' she cried, as he leapt ashore after bringing the boat alongside the jetty. There was no need to mention that she had been there all afternoon!

'Have you?' he smiled, taking hold of her.

'Yes, I have,' she gulped, startled to find she was speaking the truth.

'Good!' he laughed, his eyes lingering on the curves pushing against her thin shirt before he kissed her warmly. 'I'm sorry I was detained, but it might have been worth it for such a welcome.'

Paula hadn't realised she had returned his kiss so fiercely. Colouring a little, she eased back to look at him. His voice was teasing, but she was faintly puzzled by some difference she could sense in him. Behind the smiles and tenderness was a new hardness, she was sure. Then she frowned, deciding she was growing too sensitive where he was concerned.

'I thought you'd gone off with Miss Frank,' she confessed wryly.

'Monica?' He glanced at her, brows rising. 'Well, I did see her, but she had nothing to do with my visit to Barbados.'

It was rather a devious answer and he gave no further explanations, but Paula made herself be content. It could be a waste of time asking any more questions. If Luke wouldn't reveal what he did on the island, there wasn't much chance of getting him to tell her what he had been doing off it!

'I've brought you a present,' he murmured in her ear,

as they walked up to the house. He had an arm around her. On his other side he had slung a hessian sack, full of goods over his broad shoulders. 'Not in there,' he laughed as she looked at it curiously, 'in my pocket.'

Paula's lovely face lit up. This was one of the things she had missed most since her parents died. They had always been giving her things. 'What is it?' she asked eagerly.

'Greedy!' he teased. 'You'll have to wait until later.'

'I wish you hadn't told me!' she complained. 'Now I'll have to wait for hours, and then you might change your mind.'

'No, I won't,' he promised solemnly. 'On the other hand, you may not be prepared to accept what I've bought. It rather depends on your answer to a question I have to ask first.'

Paula felt almost too nervous and excited to dress carefully that evening for dinner. She spent the best part of an hour in the bath, trying to relax her tense nerves. The warm water did help, and after drying herself and completing the rest of her toilet, she viewed her reflection with a small gleam of satisfaction. She saw a beautiful green-eyed woman with just the exact amount of appeal she had been aiming for. If it was marriage that Luke had in mind, she doubted if he would be able to resist her.

As they had walked to the house, earlier, with her quick intelligence, Paula had guessed Luke's question would be in the nature of a proposal and his present a ring. It hadn't been difficult to work out. Of course, he could easily be stringing her along—with Luke one never knew! He wasn't the easiest of men to sum up. She licked her lips reflectively. If he was thinking of asking her to marry him and hesitating, it might pay her to give him some extra encouragement.

The shaded lights and champagne she found in the dining-room seemed to indicate that her conclusions might not be so far out. Luke was waiting for her, and glancing at his rather sober face, she decided recklessly to put her plan into immediate action. 'What are we celebrating?' she asked, bending to examine the champagne in the bucket of ice, with a taut smile. 'Your return, or my departure?'

'Departure?' Luke came to her side, looking slightly startled. 'I thought you could stay as long as you liked?'

She sighed, trying to prevent herself from drinking in every detail of his appearance and to ignore his frowning glance. She kept her eyes glued to the champagne. 'I can't stay indefinitely, Luke, and while I enjoy your company, I don't adore islands so much. And I do have a living to earn.'

He ignored everything but her third statement. 'You mean you don't like—this island?'

Managing to seem terribly uncomfortable, Paula gambled everything on one last throw. 'Not a lot,' she confessed, knowing she was either paving the way to getting him to leave Sabina, once and for all, or inviting total defeat.

# CHAPTER SIX

'WELL,' laughed Luke, 'at least you're being honest. But don't worry about the island, or getting back to work—I have other plans for you.'

His eyes were so warmly caressing that Paula thought she couldn't lose. Confidence swept over her in a jubilant wave. 'You've made me curious,' she declared with a smile, 'I can't wait to hear!'

'Later,' he said firmly. 'Here's Rose with our dinner and she won't want it spoilt. We're late enough already.'

'It's my fault,' Paula apologised charmingly to Rose. 'I forget the time.'

'You're looking beautiful tonight, Miss Paula,' Rose beamed, forgiving her.

'I'm hungry!' exclaimed Luke, pretending to be impatient as he pushed in Paula's chair.

In spite of him declaring he was hungry, Paula noticed he ate little more than she did. He seemed oddly keyed up and trying to hide it. She felt sure that he was considering proposing to her. Most men would take something like that very seriously, wouldn't they? She knew she must accept if he did propose, and, surprisingly, her former confidence was replaced by a surge of pain. What had caused it, she had no idea, but when it passed she felt horribly cold.

When Rose brought their coffee, she said good night and left them alone. Luke carried the tray into the lounge then returned for the still unopened champagne. Setting the ice-bucket down, he said slowly. 'Have there been many men in your life, Paula? I mean, men you've loved?'

'No.' She dismissed Ian. He hadn't meant a thing, and she had hated him after he had broken their engagement.

'Paula,' Luke said simply, reaching for her hand, 'how do you feel about me? How would you feel about marrying me?'

Paula stared at him. Now that the moment she had worked hard for had arrived, something clogged in her throat, preventing an immediate reply. Indescribable sensations rushed over her, like those she had experienced during dinner, making her tremble. It must be the anticlimax of something happening which she had never quite believed would.

When she should have been accepting Luke's proposal as quickly as she could, she found herself asking huskily, 'Why?'

'Why?' Her question appeared to startle him, as if he was wondering the same thing himself. Then the slightly ironical inflection in his voice disappeared and she quivered under its increased ardency. 'The usual reasons, I suppose, and because I love you.'

Luke loved her? Paula didn't know why she should feel so winded. How much more battering could she take emotionally? Yet her scepticism faded as she realised he must be speaking the truth. Love could be the only reason why he was proposing. Couldn't he get all the beauty and sex he wanted without committing himself in any way? It had to be something more powerful than merely the desire to take a woman to bed, to make him give up the freedom he valued so much for a penniless girl from London.

'Why so surprised?' he asked, when she remained silent. His eyes glittering strangely, he lifted her chin to study her pale face. 'Hasn't any man ever told you he loved you before?'

She flushed, thinking again of Ian and wishing she hadn't. 'It's not that,' she whispered, wondering where her self-confidence had gone. 'I didn't think you were the kind to fall in love, I thought you would never be that vulnerable . . .'

He smiled darkly. 'I didn't believe I was either. But how about you? How do you feel?'

Here came the crunch. He wasn't to be put off indefinitely. With surprising difficulty she forced the lie past her lips. 'I do love you, Luke . . .'

'But?'

She swallowed at his perception. 'I—I'm not sure that I could live here.'

He appeared to relax, as though relieved there was no greater problem. 'For a moment you had me worried,' he smiled. 'I'll sell Sabina, darling.'

'You—you will?'

'Stop stuttering and stammering,' he teased, bending his head to kiss her mouth. 'Umm,' he murmured reflectively, 'if it's a case of having to choose . . .'

Was that a question? Cautiously Paula rubbed a finger over lips that felt surprisingly bruised. 'I'd rather you sold it now than later.'

'Don't you trust me?'

'It's not a matter of trust,' she argued, 'Anyway, that's not quite what I meant. According to what I've heard, a lot of men promise all kinds of things before they marry, then afterwards promptly forget. I've had friends whose marriages have ended in divorce because of that.'

'So you want me to part with the island immediately?'

'There's no hurry,' she denied. 'Before we're married would do.'

In the silence that followed she was aware of Luke's sharp attention. Then he said slowly, 'I appreciate your frankness and honesty, Paula, and I won't insult you by not matching it. Sabina filled a need in my life. It helped me achieve a goal which no longer exists. I'll sell the island, and gladly. In the years to come you won't have to feel guilty over it.'

'Oh, Luke!' The mysterious tears which had so haunted her lately moistened Paula's eyes. 'I don't know what to say!'

'Shush!' He drew her closer to him, with such tenderness on his face that she wondered why his hands hurt. 'We can be happy anywhere, my darling. I know—er—someone who would take the island tomorrow. As soon as it's gone we will be married. Right?'

'That will be—wonderful!' she breathed.

He delved in his pocket, finding a box containing a ring. 'This is your present,' he confessed with a grin. 'Didn't you guess?'

She had to pretend she hadn't. 'I thought it was the champagne.'

He gave a delighted chuckle, then sobered gravely as he removed the ring from its box and slipped it on her finger. 'We can have the champagne now, as well.'

As he turned from her abruptly, to pop the cork and pour the sparkling wine into two glasses, she stared at the ring on her left hand. It was nice, but not to be compared with Ian's huge diamond, yet she gazed at it with the kind of regard she had never felt for her other ring, for a moment forgetting she was playing a game of pretence.

'It's lovely, Luke,' she whispered huskily as they drank to their future happiness.

'I'm pleased you like it.'

'Yes.' She gulped the champagne down and didn't object when he refilled her glass. She felt she needed something.

Setting their glasses aside, Luke drew her down on the sofa and began kissing her almost savagely. His arms went around her like iron bands, as though he was trying to break her in two. The fierceness of his lovemaking startled her.

'We'll be married as soon as I get rid of the island,' he gasped against her lips. 'You won't make me wait longer than that?'

'Not if you're nice to me,' she tried to tease.

'I intend treating you as you deserve, my darling.'

It could only be the role she was playing that made Paula go suddenly tense. Her eyes widened briefly at his enigmatical tones and she shifted uncomfortably.

'That sounds slightly ominous, Luke!'

He laughed against her cheek. 'I promise to beat you only once a day.'

The champagne had clouded her brain. She eased carefully away from him to give herself time to think. Pretending to be amused by his sally, she asked, 'Will you tell Rose and Henry about us?'

'Of course,' he said, his eyes wandering to her breasts.

She drew a sharp breath, wishing she had worn something more concealing, forgetting she had set out to entice. 'Will they be disappointed about the island?'

'They're very fond of it,' he admitted, 'but they don't really mind where they live.'

'Where will you—we live?'

He didn't seem to notice her small mistake. 'Wherever you fancy, love. We'll have to consider after the island's sold. You won't be marrying a man of unlimited means, my darling.'

'I don't mind being a poor man's wife,' she smiled, and was rewarded by another kiss. As his lips left hers slowly, she faltered, 'You never know what you might get for Sabina, though.'

Thoughtfully, he ran his fingers down her arm. 'I might decide to put it on the open market.'

Some alarm showed on Paula's face before she could prevent it. Such a plan wouldn't suit the Cranfords. 'We don't want to wait any longer than necessary,' she exclaimed.

'To get married, you mean?' When she nodded, he caught her closer, his eyes smouldering. 'We don't have to postpone belonging to each other, darling. It need have nothing to do with the wedding ceremony. We're engaged, remember?'

Nervously she retreated again. 'I'd rather wait, Luke. It's not that I want to,' she hastened to add, as disappointment darkened his face, 'but all these years I've been—well, saving myself for my wedding night.' Which at least was no lie!

Luke argued, 'But you've never been engaged before.'

'No . . .' How else could she answer? Mutinously she closed her eyes to the complete disintegration of her integrity. If she was to get through the next few days, she should be worrying about other things more important than that.

'Why be so old-fashioned, darling?' wheedled Luke in honeyed tones. 'You wouldn't have any regrets, I promise you.'

'How can you know?' she asked stiffly.

He tasted the sensitive skin at the corner of her mouth before his lips trailed seductively to her earlobe. 'I'm thirty-four, Paula, and I haven't led a totally celibate life. I think I'd know how to please you.'

Paula felt herself tremble. It was becoming more and more difficult to concentrate on anything but the spreading of the flame he ignited so easily inside her. The gentle movements of his hands were working a spell on her, calling on some deep, hitherto unknown element of her femininity. His eyes were begging passionately for her acquiescence, making it almost impossible for her to resist him.

'Look at me, darling, please!' The gentle, coaxing tones touched her as none of Ian's pleadings ever could. Confused, she pressed her face against his shoulder and felt his hand stroking her hair. At that moment nothing else but him seemed important.

His arms tightened around her and he whispered thickly, 'You need me, Paula. The other night I took fright at your virginity, but everything is different now, now that we've discovered we love each other. Let me show you, darling.'

His palms slipped down her arms to cup over her breasts. Pushing the top of her dress aside, he let the tips of his fingers rest on her nipples, which startled her by immediately responding, betraying her by their hardening. He made tiny circles, he followed up with his tongue, teasing her gently. 'See what I mean, darling?' he whispered huskily.

She saw all right. She felt his hot, moist breath on her cheek, then her mouth, and couldn't pretend she didn't. The blood hammered in her ears as she realised that somehow he had undermined her defences. She had allowed herself to be lured into a dangerous position through foolishly underestimating the effect he had on her.

'I'm sorry, darling,' she didn't have to try too hard to sound strained, 'I'd really rather wait.'

'You're sure?' he insisted heavily.

She stared at him for a moment, then lowered her eyes, biting her lip at the censure in his. 'Yes,' she whispered numbly.

She felt his watchful regard, then his hand was under her chin, forcing her to look at him. 'I'm too impatient, but I don't want you worrying about it. I guess I can wait if I have to, as long as I don't have to keep my hands off you completely.'

Mutely, Paula shook her head. She still felt a sense of awe that such a man had fallen in love with her. He must be one of the most superb physical specimens alive; even his brain was superior. His intelligence was such that it amazed her how easily she had fooled him. Perhaps there was some truth in the saying that love made one blind!

Believing he would wish to have more discussion on their future, she was relieved when he merely kissed her and put her aside.

'Why don't we go and make some more coffee?' he suggested, pulling her up beside him. 'Then perhaps you should have an early night.'

Paula had difficulty in getting to sleep that night although it hadn't been that early when she went to bed. They had played some records, which Luke enjoyed as much as she did as they both shared the same tastes. They hadn't talked much, but it had been almost twelve before she had gone to her room, only to lie wide awake for what had seemed like hours. Because of this, she slept late and her nerves were still in the same raw state when she woke up. She resigned herself to the indisputable fact that they might stay this way until she was safely back in London.

Even after she had showered her hands felt clammy and her body taut. The green eyes which stared back from her reflection were shadowed and dark. She had never found deceiving Luke easy, but it seemed to be getting harder. He affected her in such a way that she couldn't somehow distance herself from what she was doing any more. She just wished it was all over.

After a few minutes of reasoning with herself, of pointing out the rewards almost within her grasp, she was able to revert to her cool, level-headed self and go and find some coffee. She didn't think she could eat anything. As it was well after nine, she wasn't surprised to find Luke in the dining-room for what Rose called his elevenses; he would have had breakfast hours ago.

'Morning, darling,' he smiled, rising to kiss her and, as usual, pulling out her chair.

Paula's lips felt stiff under his, it took a lot of control not to push him away. His smile bothered her. She wasn't surprised to find she was trembling.

He bent over her, as she sat down, intent on kissing her again. He wore a pair of jeans, his shirt open to the waist. She could feel the coarse hair on his chest abrasive on the bare skin of her shoulders that the straps of her sundress didn't cover. She shuddered as he nuzzled her cheek while one of his hands moved to her closed lids, tracing the contours lightly before curling around her neck under her chin.

When his other hand grasped a strap of her dress as if he intended lowering it, she protested hoarsely. 'Luke, it's far too early!'

He looked amused and faintly puzzled as he let go. 'Darling, when we're married, I'll be making love to you all hours of the day, not just through the night. I have a very trigger-happy sexuality.'

'Yes,' she whispered, compelled to put on an act. Opening her eyes to look at him, she saw his had turned black, with a kind of hunger smouldering in them. It was as if even thinking of making love to her had been enough to drive his amusement away and half madden him. She was beginning to recognise what kind of a man he was. Once she had thought he was inclined to be austere but that had been a mistake. Now she realised that where his feelings were involved he was very easily aroused. Unfortunately he was capable of arousing her to an unbelievable degree. It couldn't be true, of course; it must be a trick. All the same, she would be glad to get back to London.

'Don't you think you're going to enjoy sex?' Luke asked, his voice whimsical as he poured them both coffee. 'You're a very passionate woman.'

She didn't believe it. 'At the moment,' she shrugged, lifting her cup to her lips, 'I'd rather have this.' Avoiding his glance, she stared moodily at her coffee which she drank without cream or sugar.

Just then the phone rang, the sound coming distantly from Luke's study, through the open door. She glanced up, startled. It seemed a strange coincidence, for she had just been about to ask him if she could use it to give her agent a ring.

'No peace for the weary,' grinned Luke. 'I'd better go and see who it is.'

Being left on her own, having time to think, didn't help her nerves. They were so bad, especially after Luke's latest remarks, that she felt like indulging in one of her old childish tantrums and throwing things. It wasn't only the present that was bothering her, it was the future. She was just beginning to be aware that Luke could be dangerous and it might not be as easy to get rid of him, after he had sold the island, as she had thought. That might be the most complicated operation of the lot, and she wondered apprehensively how she was going to manage it.

He returned quietly, while she was still deep in thought, which in no way prepared her for the bombshell he was about to drop. When he said, quite casually, 'That was Denis Cranford on the phone,' she nearly died of shock.

'D-Denis Cranford?'

'Yes,' Luke's tone didn't alter, 'He wants to know if you've managed to persuade me to sell Sabina yet. I told him he'd better speak to you.'

'B-but I can't!' Paula went on stammering, her face sheet-white. 'He had no right . . .!'

'You can and you will!' Luke's hand shot out, as if to drag her to his study, but taking one look at his furious face, Paula promptly fainted.

When she came round, she was lying on the sofa with Luke trickling cold water on her.

'Ah, so you've recovered,' he exclaimed, scarcely giving her time to, before he began hurling further accusations at her. 'I should have guessed you were in league with that scoundrel. Not that I'll be the first man to be taken in by a pretty face!'

The contempt in his voice was shattering. Paula went completely to pieces. Hoarsely she whispered, 'What are you going to do?'

'Plenty!' he snapped, terrifying her further.

How could the Cranfords have done this to her! Moaning, she hid her face in her hands, unsure whether the dampness she encountered was tears of anguish or the water Luke had been pouring over her. 'They promised you wouldn't know!' she choked, unwittingly, partly due to shock, giving everything away.

There was a long, pregnant silence which seemed suddenly to be pounding into her almost physically. Panic-stricken, she looked up. 'The phone!' she gasped, still too confused to think properly.

Luke was watching her coldly, only a pulse beating in his jaw revealing that he felt like murder. 'That wasn't Denis Cranford on the phone,' he said flatly. 'It was Henry, ringing from Barbados.'

Paula stared at him, horror slowly dawning on her face as the full implications of what Luke was saying got through to her and she began working things out. 'You tricked me!' she cried wildly.

For a moment, after her outburst, she thought he was going to strike her. His hands were still clenched as he backed away.

'My, God, you have a nerve to accuse me of that,' he snapped, 'when you came here deliberately to trick me! And had it not been for my cousin on Barbados, your deplorable little scheme might have worked.'

While Paula groped for words she couldn't find, he went on harshly, 'A lot of people have wanted Sabina, but the Cranfords offered most. If all had gone according to plan—your plan—I might have proposed, genuinely proposed,' he emphasised grimly. 'Not that charade I conducted last night—And within a very short time, I have no doubt, I'd have been deprived of the island as well as my wife! How long did you intend staying with me after Sabina had gone, Paula?'

Paula was trembling. She felt she had been dealt a knock-out blow. Luke seemed to know it all. A wave of blackness threatened, but she fought it off. Whatever happened she mustn't faint again. 'I can explain, Luke,' she choked.

'What?' he snarled, eyes black with rage. 'It might make interesting hearing, but I've no stomach for more of your lies, the excuses I imagine you've prepared to meet the unlikely contingency of my discovering what you were up to. By putting two and two together, I don't need to listen to any explanations of yours. I know what happened, and what I don't know I can guess.'

'You could be wrong,' she retorted.

'No,' he bit out. 'And I don't think any purpose can be served by talking about it. I'm as furious with myself as I am with you—no man appreciates being made a fool of. When the Cranfords sent a woman to do their dirty work, I fell for one of the oldest tricks in the book!'

Paula croaked, as the pain in her throat affected her

voice. 'You can at least tell me how you found out! If you haven't been in touch with the Cranfords . . .'

'Why not?' he rasped sarcastically. 'It might do you no harm to realise you need a lot more expertise before you try your hand at this kind of thing again.'

As she flinched, he looked at her contemptuously. 'If anything's to blame for the failure of your plans, it might be the small fiasco that occurred at Peter's hotel, the day your team—or were they your confederates?—left to go home. That morning, for various reasons, three of his receptionists failed to turn up, which was how he happened to be on the desk, helping out, when a man rang from the U.K. asking to speak to you. He put him through.

'The man's voice,' Luke went on, 'had tickled his imagination ever since. It had a slight hesitation, and it got so that he was determined to remember who it belonged to. When it came to him that he had been speaking to Denis Cranford, he didn't know what to do.'

'How could he be sure?' Paula gasped.

'He couldn't,' Luke retorted icily. 'The Cranfords had stayed in the hotel twice while they were trying to buy this island, but their secretary had made the reservations. He'd had no communication with either brothers over the phone. It was just a hunch he felt eventually compelled to act on.'

'So he called you,' Paula muttered sullenly. 'That's where you were the other day?'

'How did you guess?' he jeered mockingly. 'Peter told me of his suspicions reluctantly, as they involved you. Which was why he wanted to see me alone. We certainly didn't discuss you, but I spent the rest of the morning thinking.'

'That must have been enlightening,' Paula began scornfully, but was silenced by another annihilating glance.

'It was,' he grated derisively. 'I started remembering several things that should have made me suspicious long ago. Such as you moaning about being broke and then suddenly having the kind of money it takes to stay in a Caribbean luxury hotel. Then you accept my invitation to come here, but every time I touch you, you freeze up. Please don't attempt to deny it, Paula,' he grated, as she opened indignant lips. 'In my kind of business I have to know women. In coming to Sabina, you were forcing yourself to accepting a degree of intimacy you didn't want. It wasn't the island that was bugging you so much, it was me.'

Luke paused, his mouth twisting derisively. 'Then, because I was still trying to give you the benefit of the doubt and even then that didn't seem sufficient evidence to go on, I rang a firm in London whose services can be relied on completely. I had to wait overnight, but they supplied me with the information I needed to fill in the gaps. Your parents left you penniless when they died eight months, not four years ago, but you continued living in style, doing little work. Your apartment is mortgaged from Cranford Brothers Ltd, and until recently you were engaged to a well known London rake. So, my dear Paula, it all began to add up. Not everything, of course. I still don't know how you intended getting rid of me after I'd handed the island over, but we'll come to that eventually.'

Paula couldn't believe anyone would go to the lengths Luke had gone to. 'How dare you have me investigated?' she demanded furiously. 'It wasn't as if the Cranfords were trying to rob you of your damned island! They were going to pay you every penny you asked for it.'

'Do you think that excuses your part in it?' he rasped, just as furiously. 'The Cranfords no longer interest me, but you do. You lied and cheated your way in here for personal gain.'

'I was desperate for money!' Paula sought to justify herself. 'I had to do something.'

'Why not an honest day's work?' he asked grimly. 'You turned down modelling jobs all the time, you were that lazy.'

God, he hadn't left a stone unturned! Enraged, she glared at him. 'It wasn't easy to adapt to a life of slavery after my parents died. I got behind with my mortgage and other payments.'

'You could have tried moving out of your luxury apartment into a room,' he suggested sarcastically.

'A—room!' she shuddered in revulsion. 'That might be all right for the likes of you.'

Clearly incensed, Luke retorted, 'I've lived in places you mightn't know existed, but I didn't owe anything. Nor did I resort to trickery and deception to get where I am today.'

'You don't have to set yourself up as a paragon of virtue,' she retorted bitterly. 'Besides, you've only got as far as this miserable little island . . .'

He ignored this, though his eyes blackened with rage. 'What happened to Ian Doobray?' he mocked savagely. 'Did he see through you as well, or did he just tire of you after he'd had his fill? And I don't doubt for a moment that he had. His reputation stinks!'

'Well, he never had me!' Paula denied angrily. 'If my parents hadn't left me destitute . . .'

'Ah,' Luke clipped in jeering, 'so now you're pretending it was just your money he was after?'

Clenching her lips, she refused to talk about it. 'It's none of your business.'

'While you craved the title he would have been able to bestow on you, should your marriage have lasted that long. Sex and gain on both sides, but no love.'

He made it sound so sordid that her hand shot out, before she could stop herself, to contact his cheek. The slap she landed on his hard face echoed loudly, but did nothing to alleviate her green-eyed fury.

He caught her wrist before she could hit him again. 'You'll regret that,' he rasped, 'a hundred times over before I'm through with you!'

'I—I won't be here,' she gasped defiantly, pain leaping up her arm from his crucifying fingers.

'Don't count on it,' his breath rasped in an obvious

attempt to control his fury. 'But before we begin to think of punishment, I'd like a few more answers, if you please. I can guess the general set up with the Cranfords, but you haven't told me yet what they were paying you.'

'Why should I,' she retorted defiantly, 'so you can crow over what I won't be getting?'

'Tell me!' he demanded implacably, twisting her wrist until she almost screamed.

'A measly few thousand,' she gulped through taut lips, 'and the deeds of my flat.'

'You were willing to commit perjury for that?'

'Do you have to put the worst construction on everything?' she cried stormily. 'I only saw it as a practical way of doing something about my straitened circumstances.'

'Some people manage to do that honestly.'

He was being so righteous that fresh fury welled in Paula's breast, driving her to lift her free hand with obvious intentions.

'I shouldn't,' Luke warned softly, eyes glittering. 'Violence has a strange way of begetting violence—and believe me, mine is barely under control.'

Fright at something in his glance shot through her, though she was determined not to let him see how scared she was.

'V-very well,' she said stiffly, 'I'll admit you've won. You can keep your damned island, I never want to see either you or it again. But just remember this, when you're seeking to condemn me. You brought me here for the sole purpose of seducing me—which can't show you in a very good light, either.'

'My God,' he snarled contemptuously, 'that has to be the joke of the century! Seducing you, when you must have lost count, long ago, of the men you've gone to bed with!'

Paula could have killed him. She didn't dare lift a finger, but she hoped the hate in her eyes told him exactly what she was thinking! 'I haven't slept with a man yet,' she said coldly. 'And another thing—you insist on calling me lazy while you don't appear to know the first thing about work yourself.'

'Don't I?'

'I've been here two weeks, remember.'

'So you have,' he returned suavely, 'and I'd no idea your opinion of me was so bad. During the next few weeks I must do my best to change it.'

'The—next few weeks?'

'Don't look so startled, Miss Edison,' he mocked. 'You didn't think you were going anywhere, did you?'

Paula felt her face grow pale as she stared at him uncertainly. 'I think this has all gone too far. There's no sense in standing here trading insults. You can take me to Barbados immediately. I'll stay at the hotel overnight and arrange to go straight back to London.'

Luke's eyes glittered again with fury. 'You take some beating!' he snapped. 'Dishing out orders, without a please or thank you, as though I'm the one in the wrong. You're just a spoilt little brat, and I'd be failing in my duty towards mankind if I didn't try and do something about it. For the next few weeks you'll be staying here with me, until you've seen the error of your ways, perhaps.'

'Are you mad?' she exclaimed imperiously. 'I'll ask Henry to take me to Barbados, if you won't.'

'Henry's not here,' he replied, 'neither is Rose. They left for New York this morning—Rose's sister is ill and asking to see her. Rose didn't hesitate when she knew you'd be around to look after me.'

'Look after you?' Paula repeated incredulously.

'You heard.'

But she still couldn't believe it. Rose and Henry gone, she alone with Luke, entirely at his mercy. For the first time she knew real fear. 'This amounts to kidnapping,' she accused desperately. 'You can't do it!'

'Don't presume to tell me what I can or cannot do!' he bit out. 'From now on you will take over all Rose's duties, which includes the cooking. I have breakfast at six-thirty and I'll expect lunch and dinner at the usual times. And it doesn't improve my temper to be kept waiting.'

'You can't make me!' Paula cried furiously, green eyes flashing. 'I'll find someone to help me get away from here somehow. There's the phone . . .'

'Disconnected.'

'A boat might call.'

'No one calls,' he retorted, with frightening emphasis. 'People know they aren't welcome unless invited.'

'Strangers might,' she muttered incoherently.

The way Luke grasped her shoulder proved his patience was running out. 'You'd be well advised to leave strangers and everyone else out of this,' he snapped, 'unless it's publicity you're after. The police are always interested in women like you, so are the media.'

'The—media!' she whispered, going white. She'd had enough of the press to last her a lifetime.

'Sure,' he taunted unmercifully. 'What wouldn't they give for a detailed account of the weeks we've spent here, just you and me, alone together on a Caribbean island.'

'They wouldn't believe such a story!' she said fiercely. 'Especially coming from someone they've never heard of before.'

'Oh, they've heard of me all right,' Luke drawled mockingly. 'If you're as genuinely fond of books as you pretend to be, you might even have heard of me yourself. My pen name happens to be Richard Ryan.'

Paula could only gape for a few seconds, like a stranded fish. 'N-not *the* R-Richard Ryan?' she stammered, 'the man who wrote *Zeta*?'

Luke nodded.

'And all those plays, films . . .'

'Right again.'

Overwhelmed by shock, Paula stared at him. 'It can't be,' she gasped. 'It's unbelievable!'

'I don't intend putting myself out to prove it,' he shrugged. 'Whether you believe it or not is up to you.'

She gulped, suddenly knowing it was true, yet she still found it difficult to take in. 'Why did you never say?'

Staring at her narrowly, he grasped the soft skin of her shoulders before he almost savagely thrust her away. 'It didn't seem important—or relevant.'

'Richard Ryan . . .' she muttered aloud, unconsciously regaining her balance. She had read all his books, powerful modern thrillers, nearly impossible to put down. Luke must be one of the most famous writers living, and published throughout the world. All those hours he spent in his study and she had never guessed who he was or what he was doing. What a fool she had been! If the press ever discovered she was alone with him here, they would have a field day!

## CHAPTER SEVEN

REALISING she was standing chewing her lip, Paula glanced at Luke's face, catching the derisive glint in his grey eyes. 'Why don't you use your real name?' she asked.

'Richard and Ryan are my other Christian names,' he replied curtly. 'I wasn't twenty when my first book was published. It wasn't up to much and I must have felt I needed something to hide behind.'

'Was it a success?'

'Surprisingly it was, which seemed to make it impossible to write under any other name.'

Paula frowned as something else puzzled her. 'When you're so famous, why do you choose to live here?'

He seemed dryly amused by the incredulity in her voice. 'I bought Sabina from a man who got no further than putting the telephone in. I've used the island as a retreat ever since.'

'The Cranfords said you'd considered selling it?'

'One day I will, but not yet.'

'And last night?' she challenged unsteadily. 'Your marriage proposal, everything, was merely to fool me?'

'Don't you think it was my turn?' he demanded silkily.

Their brief truce, during which they had discussed his writing, was over. Paula glared at him as she flushed a guilty pink. 'Well, I don't intend staying here to run after you! You can get Rose back as quick as you like, unless you intend looking after yourself. I'm going to pack!'

'Oh no, you don't, lady!' he snapped, catching hold of her as she turned, 'You'll do exactly as I say or you'll never dare show your face again, either in London or elsewhere!'

'Threats!' she retorted, eyes blazing scornfully.

For an answer Luke pulled her completely into his arms and lowered his mouth to crush hers with a violence she couldn't escape. The angry retort she had uttered was crushed into silence against his lips as he forced her to yield. She tried to resist him, but as he held her ruthlessly, her body went limp and she trembled against the powerful hardness of his male frame. A shiver of shock shot up her spine and she couldn't suppress her racing thoughts. She felt part of him. Despite his cruelty, she wanted him. Wildly she wrenched away from him, feeling she must be going out of her mind.

'D—don't dare do that again!' she stammered, her face burning.

'I won't,' he glared back, 'if you heed my warning. Otherwise,' he snapped, 'you know what you're inviting!'

During the next few days, Paula began to be actually certain she was going out of her mind. If the job she had been doing for the Cranfords had bothered her, it didn't seem half as bad as the one she was doing now.

After her confrontation with Luke, she had sat in her room and sulked until he had stormed in and dragged her out after reading her another lecture. When he finished, she supposed he had put what was commonly known as the fear of death into her, because she hadn't dared defy him again. It didn't seem possible, but she found herself obeying his every command, with a subservience that appeared to gratify him but which she didn't understand.

She rose at six each morning and worked hard throughout the entire day. Sometimes when she glanced in a mirror, which she did less and less frequently, she scarcely recognised the tousle-haired creature who gazed back at her.

No longer was she immaculately made-up and groomed. Her hair was a riot of tumbled curls, her face scrubbed clean even of lipstick—that just melted while she was working, anyway. The enervating heat had sweat constantly trickling down her body as she cooked and made beds and polished floors. Even when she left her shirt unbuttoned indecently low, it didn't help much.

Yet she soon became indifferent to her appearance. She had Luke's huge house to take care of and she couldn't take care of both! And when she tumbled into bed at night, she was more concerned for her aching limbs than how she looked.

Sometimes she viewed the whole scene with a sense of total unreality, sure that she would wake up and find she had dreamt it all, but she never did. Luke was an unrelenting taskmaster; he complained all the time if everything was not entirely to his liking. He was incredulous when she told him she had never swept a floor and had been openly derisive when she had confessed that she had had a woman who came in for two hours each day to clean her flat for her.

'You're the charwoman here,' he had laughed, hauling her inhumanely from her room, one evening, when she had failed to wash the dinner dishes. 'You'd better get on with them,' he'd thrust her nose in the sink. 'It doesn't bother me whether you get any sleep or not, but I won't have an untidy kitchen!'

Then he demanded breakfast at an hour she hadn't know existed. 'What's to stop you getting your own?' she had groused when after two mornings he refused to put up with what he called 'her laziness' any longer.

'I don't cook my own breakfast because I have other things to do,' he retorted curtly. 'If you're too damn lazy to get out of bed by yourself, tomorrow I intend coming to help you.'

That did it. Every morning after that Paula was up at six. She couldn't bear the thought of his hands on her again and he'd have no compunction over hauling her out of bed half naked. Every time she remembered what it had been like to be that near him, a terrible feeling came over her, weakening her already low reserves, making her want to weep. She didn't know why she was so torn, these days, between anger and tears. Luke hated her, the Cranfords had deserted her, having apparently taken Luke's word when he had informed them by phone that the deal was off. No one obviously cared enough to come and rescue her. The Cranfords would be still worrying over Luke's threat to their image, while she, seemingly, hadn't a friend in the world!

Luke had taken his ring back, which had depressed her even further, as it appeared to end everything, whether make-believe or otherwise between them. He had laughed and said it must be one of the shortest engagements on record, yet behind his mocking remark she had sensed a continuing anger. She supposed while he felt like this, he wouldn't let her go, but sometimes, when her back ached in conjunction with her heart, she hoped it wouldn't be long.

She was still stunned about him being a famous writer. Once she had learned who he was, she began recalling seeing photographs of him which confirmed he was indeed Richard Ryan. It was because she hadn't known what he did that she hadn't connected him with the man whose face must be familiar to thousands. Wistfully she wondered about the book he was writing now, that kept him closeted for such long hours in his study, but she didn't dare ask.

For days now he had ignored her. If ever he threw a word in her direction, it was rarely a civil one, and the tension in the air was getting her down. Both her temper and nerves were wearing thin. She didn't eat her meals with him any more, though that was maybe her own fault. She had told him she would have hers in the kitchen, as a matter of pride, but had felt slightly put out when he hadn't argued. It wasn't until after her outburst that she had realised that if she didn't see him at mealtimes, she might never see him at all.

It was after she had taken his coffee in, one evening, and was standing by the kitchen window unhappily drinking her own, that she noticed the boat. She had been thinking of Luke and she must have been staring at it for some time without actually seeing it. It wasn't too close inshore, but it might be near enough to see her if she waved. Impulsively disregarding Luke's orders, she hurried to the door, unfortunately missing the table with her cup, which crashed to the floor. The noise must have alerted Luke, for he was almost immediately behind her as she ran outside.

She only managed one wave before his arms closed around her. 'What the hell do you think you're doing?' he snarled.

'Trying to attract the attention of the people in that boat!' she gasped, struggling wildly.

He laughed harshly, his arms tightening until she couldn't move a limb. Then shock and dizziness coursed through her as he began kissing her passionately before picking her up and carrying her back in the house.

'Anyone watching us,' he taunted, 'will immediately take us for lovers, or a couple on their honeymoon. It will certainly discourage them from intruding.'

'You think you're very clever, don't you?' she mumbled childishly, when he let her draw breath. 'Well, you're mistaken. You might keep me here and treat me like a servant, but that's about all you can do. You don't impress me one bit! You may have made a name for yourself, but before that what were you? Nothing!'

Meeting her blazing eyes, he rasped, 'So you don't believe I'm good enough to lick your boots?'

His face was hard, his eyes black with fury. His anger had returned with a force that should have warned her to pause. Her eyes were blinded, however, by the tears of her own anger, while in her ears his furious voice was little more than a blur. Contemptuous words poured from her lips, she didn't seem able to stop. She either had to love Luke, or hate him! Dear God, she couldn't be in danger of succumbing to the former? She couldn't stop herself from thinking about him. During the night, he absorbed all her sleepless thoughts. The knowledge of her own vulnerability burst upon her like an avalanche, stunning her into near hysterics.

'Let me go!' she cried, and groaned. 'You aren't fit to touch me!'

It might have been the way her green eyes flashed with a fiery disdain that exploded the crumbling remnants of the control Luke had been exercising for days. It snapped as his vengeful arms threatened to remove the last breath from her body, as he carried her swiftly to her bedroom. 'Before I'm through with you,' he rasped, 'you'll be just about ready to crawl!'

Paula felt herself being flung on her bed. Earlier she had showered, but she hadn't changed for dinner since she had been forced to cook it; it hadn't seemed worth the bother. Tonight she was wearing shorts, because the evening was hot, but he simply ripped them off.

'Now scream for mercy,' he jeered, his hands lifting her bare thighs so he had room to lie down beside her.

As his mouth took hers, Paula realised her breath should be saved for more important things than screaming. 'You must be mad if you think you can get away with this!' she panted against his lips, trying to escape him.

'I've been warning you for days,' he retorted, taking her defiant lower lip between his teeth and biting.

'You're always warning me about something!' she cried painfully, when she was able to speak.

Luke's eyes were still black with fury. 'You refused to recognise the danger of driving me too far.'

She tried to free one of her hands to hit him, but he held her too tightly. 'You're nothing but the lowest of the low!' she hissed furiously.

'Well, well,' he leered mockingly, 'the lady in you is certainly coming out! You wouldn't deprive a nobody of possessing somebody, just once in his life, would you? Not when you've always been so generous with other men.'

Fear began mingling with the fire shooting through her as she recognised the ruthlessness behind Luke's

taunting tones. Somehow he had managed to remove
all their clothing without releasing her an inch, and she
felt a strange heat consuming her as she closed her eyes
against the hard nakedness of his tall, powerful body.
He was the first man who had ever made her feel
helpless and feminine, and it was amazing how well her
smaller limbs fitted into his. She had only to tip her
head back to allow their lips to meet.

Her face burning at such thoughts galvanised her into
action. She began fighting again in real earnest
although with no more success than before. Luke put a
stop to it immediately by renewing his assault on her
mouth while continuing to hold her in a grip of iron.
Paula's breasts were crushed against his chest and her
hips were pulled intimately close to his as he forced her
lips apart.

Paula's breathing became so rapid it roared in her
ears, while her heart threatened to beat out of her body.
She gasped as her nipples hardened to the roughness of
his palms, and the familiar drowning sensation she felt
when she was close to him was like a powerful current
sweeping her near to disaster. How could she fight her
own treacherous instincts? From the feelings coursing
through her the battle was already lost, yet if she didn't
manage to do something would she ever be able to face
herself again?

Frantically she squirmed, but the more she rolled and
thrashed across the bed, the more savage enjoyment
Luke appeared to derive from it. Ruthlessly he followed
her every move until, tiring of it, he imprisoned her
brutally beneath the weight of his muscular thighs.
Paula had never known such a mixture of fear and
passion, and she was rapidly losing the strength to
prevent herself from being overwhelmed by the latter.
Her limbs refused to heed the frenzied instructions of
her brain to help her resist the terrible danger she was
in. Luke and she were battling, but like a pair of ill-
assorted antagonists, and she was no match for him.

In the end she could no longer oppose the onslaught

of his powerful body, the kisses he rained on what seemed like every inch of her. When his mouth finally closed over hers and stayed, she laced her fingers through his dark hair, like an act of fevered assent.

'I want you,' her hungry heart whispered at one juncture, but she had no idea the words had escaped her shaken lips.

Luke didn't answer. He was breathing harshly, his tightening arms proving his desires were as wild as her own. His body was urging, tormenting, inciting, as their arms and mouths fought to relieve the feelings mounting intolerably inside them. Paula's heart was racing and there was white hot fire in her blood making her dizzy and breathless. She trembled from the sheer force of it.

When Luke's hand parted her thighs, finding her ready and waiting for him, she sucked in her breath. But when he slipped in between them as his body covered her, she cried out. Their joining wasn't gentle and it brought a brief stab of pain, but though he paused, it was quickly lost in the tumult of emotion he was arousing. She wouldn't have believed the rapturous pleasure he was stirring within her was possible. Always she had been convinced she was frigid, and the released force of her own passion came as a great shock. She could feel it building up inside her until she was writhing in Luke's arms under the force of it. Blindly she clutched convulsively at the damp flesh of his back and shoulders as every bit of her responded to him with an urgency she couldn't restrain.

She shuddered with delight as Luke answered her unspoken plea, but there was more to come. As he uttered her name with a hoarse cry of exultation, in the same instant an explosion erupted inside her that triggered off an ever-widening succession of shock waves, beginning in her limbs and spreading throughout her body with such a soul-shattering force of ecstasy she almost lost consciousness. The spiral of fulfilment seemed to go on for ever and ended at last in an explosion of showering stars.

She didn't pass out, but afterwards she was aware of nothing but a sense of peace and the relaxed heaviness of Luke's limbs. She was still in a dream world that had no connection with harsh reality. Luke made no attempt to move and she didn't know how long they stayed locked in each other's arms. She kept thinking that none of this could be possible, that any moment she would wake up and find it hadn't happened. It was difficult to credit she was capable of responding to any man as she had done to Luke.

She had to believe it, though, as throughout the night he made love to her again and again. Her face and body burned with his kisses, as he left not an inch of her unexplored. It seemed they were moving through an enchanted period of sensuous hours with no thought beyond the present. Luke's skilful mouth rained kisses on her everywhere, scorching her lips, her eyes and cheeks, the soft hollows of her throat, and time and time again he brought her to a consuming peak of rapture that continually seemed to reach new heights. He didn't seem as if he could get enough of her or deny himself the incredible degree of pleasure he was deriving from her now uninhibited and wholehearted response.

The next morning when Paula woke she was alone. For a few minutes after realising Luke had gone, she lay still, trying dreamily to recapture what had taken place during the night. Luke wasn't with her, but he had made love to her, he had at last made her aware of what it was like to be a woman. Recalling his lovemaking, she felt no sense of shame, only warm fulfilment. Sometime in the night, she knew she had grown up, and not just because she had surrendered herself to him. She had thought she hated Luke Armstrong, now she knew beyond doubt that she loved him. She had believed she was frigid, incapable of loving anyone; it brought relief and joy to know differently. The trouble all along had been, she suspected, that she was basically a woman who could only respond to one man. Not every woman had this problem—if it could be called a problem—but she

had, For her there had to be love before she could
indulge in sex. She must be one of the lucky few that
she had found it, and, in doing so, had been privileged
to discover the deep well of passion inside herself.

All her doubts were suddenly gone. Luke hadn't been
gentle with her, but she owed him a debt of gratitude.
This morning she saw herself as a different person, no
longer the shallow, self-absorbed girl she had been up
until now. She was reluctant to think about it too
deeply, for her transformation promised to be somewhat
overwhelming, but she knew she might be changed
beyond recognition.

Wincing a little wryly but not regretting the bruises
that made her body ache slightly, Paula left her bed. It
was just after six, but instead of feeling weighed down
by her usual depression, she felt ready for anything. It
was imperative that she find Luke, to tell him how
happy she was and to apologise for everything. He must
like her a little or he wouldn't have brought her here in
the first place, she decided optimistically. Perhaps he
might actually love her as much as she loved him and
was just waiting for a sign before he told her so. Her
heart danced with happiness.

After her shower she dressed quickly, almost
throwing on her shirt and cotton pants. Today she
didn't need any make-up to make her face glow. Her
green eyes shone softly, her hair was a mass of colour,
her mouth a warm, seductive pink, just waiting to be
kissed. She saw in astonishment that she looked quite
radiantly beautiful, and for Luke's sake she was
pleased.

Usually in the mornings she made a pot of coffee
which Luke liked to drink while she cooked his
breakfast. She was disappointed that he wasn't around
when she first went out, but by the time the coffee was
percolating she heard him in the dining-room. Taking
in the coffee, she smiled at him shyly.

'Good morning,' she said softly.

He was sitting carelessly at the table reading a

magazine and scarcely glanced up to acknowledge her. He merely nodded absently.

'It's a lovely morning,' she persevered, staring at him eagerly.

As the weather was nice most days, she wasn't surprised when he ignored her remark, but she felt hurt when he said curtly, again without raising his eyes, 'I'd appreciate breakfast as soon as possible, Paula. I've a lot of work to get through.'

'Of course,' she gulped, shooting him another uncertain glance before retreating back to the kitchen. He hadn't said a word about last night. He was treating her exactly the same as he had yesterday. She had thought he might take her in his arms and kiss her, but he hadn't even looked at her properly!

Taking a deep breath, Paula clenched cold hands. Hadn't she better get this properly in perspective before she said or did something foolish? Luke was used to her ranting and sulking. She had cheated and lied to him, she couldn't expect him to believe she had changed overnight. She would have to prove she had before he learned to trust her again. It occurred to her that his faith in her might never be renewed, but with a sob she realised that if she was impatient now she might spoil everything.

While she cooked his breakfast, she found it helped to keep her mind on what she was doing. She must remember to transfer some bacon from the deep-freeze to the fridge, otherwise there would be none for tomorrow morning's breakfast. She grilled Luke four rashers together with sausages and tomatoes and fried him two eggs which she put on a tray with a pile of toast and carried to him.

'Thanks,' he said briefly.

She hovered tentatively, wondering if he might ask her to join him this morning, but although he did look at her eventually, his grey eyes were bleak and there was certainly no invitation of any kind in them. He was wearing light slacks with an open-necked shirt. He looked fit and healthy, but his face was an iron mask. Sharply she turned her head to watch the sun coming up over the horizon, turning the sea into a sheet of glittering colour. The beauty of it brought a lump to Paula's throat. Again she was acutely aware of Luke's presence beside her, and the feeling of tension between them made her tremble. For a moment she was tempted to speak of their lovemaking during the night, but finding it difficult to even mention it, she decided to leave it. She wasn't sure what she could say about it, anyway.

'I'll fetch some more coffee,' she muttered, thinking it would be an excuse to come back, but he told her not to bother.

'I've enough here,' he said, indicating his still full cup.

'If you're sure,' she responded with another nervous smile as she left him, unable to find an excuse to linger any longer.

In the kitchen she tried to eat her own breakfast. Lately, all the work she had been doing, together with the anger she had felt against Luke and life in general, had given her quite an appetite, but today she didn't feel hungry. Luke was clearly wary. He wasn't going to forgive her in a hurry. As the knowledge sank in, Paula wiped a furtive tear from her eye. It would take time.

She spent the rest of the morning getting through her usual amount of housework then preparing lunch. She did her chores with more interest this morning, suddenly finding pleasure in making Luke's house look nice. She even went outside and picked a large bunch of flowers from the garden, which she arranged in vases in the lounge and hall. They might soon wilt, but they did give the rather austere rooms a brighter, more welcoming appearance. Having seen some gay cotton material in Rose's storeroom one day, while she was searching for dusters, she wondered if she would be any good at sewing. The lounge might be even more transformed by new curtains and covers, if she could manage to make them.

When Luke didn't leave his study for lunch, she put some soup and sandwiches on a tray and carried it to him. His study was at the back of the house, down a long passage. She sighed when she thought of how long the passage seemed when she cleaned it.

'Come in,' he called as she knocked, and when he saw what she was carrying he frowned. 'I don't know that I have time to stop.'

'You'll work better,' she tried to speak lightly, 'if you have something to eat.'

'Thanks,' he said briefly, as she placed the tray on the desk beside him. 'Another time, if I want anything, I'll come out.'

He wasn't being particularly gracious. Paula glanced over the tray she had set with such care and sighed, 'I'm sorry.'

His eyes flicked over her, lingering on her taut breasts until, as if suddenly aware of what he was doing, his mouth tightened and he glanced away. 'There's no need to apologise,' he snapped harshly.

When Luke was in a bad mood she knew better than to argue. Without looking at him again, she made for the door, but before she could reach it he stopped her.

'Wait a minute,' he ordered abruptly, 'I want to talk to you.'

She supposed he intended talking about the night they had spent together, at last, and a faint flush mounted her pale cheeks, but instead he said coolly, 'I wasn't going to mention the subject again, but we never went into your financial arrangements with the Cranfords very deeply.'

Paula gazed at him in consternation. She wished he hadn't asked. After what had happened, she felt too ashamed to talk about it. Endeavouring to put him off, she replied awkwardly, 'I think I've told you most of it.'

'But not all of it,' he retorted.

'Very well,' she agreed, staring at the floor, reluctant to meet the condemnation in his eyes. 'If I succeeded in persuading you to sell Sabina, they were going to write off my mortgage and throw in a few thousand, as I've already told you. If I failed, they agreed to pay my fare home and my mortgage to the end of the year.'

'They made it an offer hard to resist. You couldn't lose.'

Paula gulped, looking at him quickly. She had an urge to confess how filled with remorse she was that she had allowed herself to be drawn into such a scheme, but the hardness of Luke's face seemed to preclude any plea on her own behalf.

'Another thing,' he spoke so musingly, as to entirely disguise the deadly content of his next query. 'If you had succeeded, how were you to get rid of me afterwards? I believe I asked you that before, but you didn't answer.'

'I don't know,' Paula's face had a hunted expression. 'I never did get things worked out as far as that.'

'A lack of proper attention to detail which could have proved your downfall,' he mocked sarcastically. 'Before you embark on your next attempt to defraud . . .'

'I've already told you I won't!' she broke in fervently.

'Before you do,' he overrode inexorably, 'you should learn never to leave anything to chance.'

'I suppose this is how you write your books?' she said irrationally. 'Nothing overlooked from the start!'

'No,' he replied curtly. 'Sometimes, when I begin one, I have no more than the main characters and a few relevant details worked out. Things usually fall into place as I go along, but you couldn't afford to take such a risk. What would you have done if you'd suddenly discovered yourself married to me, for instance?'

'Oh . . .' she floundered, her face flushing wildly, 'I— well, there's always divorce . . .'

'Didn't you realise,' he continued unmercifully, 'if you'd played your cards right and not made so many foolish mistakes . . .'

'M—mistakes?'

'Such as forgetting to ring Denis Cranford, so he was forced to ring you,' Luke explained, with icy impatience. 'You might have feathered your nest even further by living with me. I'm really quite a wealthy man, Paula. You might have gained a lot.'

'I couldn't have done that!' she exclaimed, recalling how she had had to force herself even to think about it. Now she felt differently. Now she might be willing to live anywhere with Luke, if only she could stay with him.

He interrupted her thoughts with a dangerous softness. 'You don't believe I would ever have genuinely proposed, do you? I'll admit I considered having an affair with you, but marriage—never!'

Paula bit her lip miserably. Where did she go from here? He was making it clearer every minute that she had no part in his future plans. Despite his ardour through the night, he despised her. He had been motivated by a desire for revenge, while for her it had been love. She could never hope now that he would ever come to love her. Even so, she would be content with whatever he was prepared to give her. To be his mistress, even for a short time, might be better than nothing.

'I realise that,' she replied in a low voice. 'And even if you had been prepared, or wanted to marry me, I don't think I could have gone through with it, without telling you the truth.'

'Well, we'll never know, will we?' he jeered.

She couldn't bear him being so angry with her again, so she gulped and nodded, and after managing to compose herself a little, while he stared at her belligerently, she said—if he didn't want her for anything else, she thought she would go for a swim.

With a wave of dismissal, he snapped, 'As long as you don't forget you have work to do.'

'I won't,' she promised quietly. 'I should only be gone an hour.'

'Take care,' he warned.

Paula treasured those two words, even if they sounded torn from him, for a long time. After changing

into her swimsuit, she decided to have her lunch outside
and carried it down to the beach. She swam first, then
ate the sandwich she had saved while making Luke's,
then finished off with an apple and a drink of
homemade lemonade. By the time she had finished
eating, her swimsuit had dried and she moved further
into the shade of the big palm tree under which she was
sitting, so she could relax for a few more minutes where
it was cooler before going back to the house. The air
and her swim had made her sleepy and her eyes began
to droop as she sat watching the sea. The next thing she
knew, Luke was shaking her awake.

He was doing it quite gently, but his voice held a note
of urgency. 'Paula!' he was saying, 'are you all right?'

She gulped and sat up, her eyes drowsy, then startled.
'I'm sorry,' she gasped, as his hands fell from her
shoulders, 'I didn't mean to fall asleep.'

'It doesn't matter,' he said roughly, 'now that I've
found you. I came out for a cup of tea and you were
nowhere to be seen. I thought something must have
happened to you.'

'I didn't get much sleep last night,' she said vaguely,
only half aware of what she was saying as their eyes
met. The longing to feel Luke cradling her in his arms,
kissing her, caressing her body, made her breathless and
so dizzy that she just babbled anything.

She almost flinched when she saw the look of utter
fury in his eyes and felt his barely suppressed rage
scorching her. What on earth had made her remind him
of that! Scrabbling to her feet, she pulled her cotton
cover-up over her swimsuit, wincing as dried-on sand
scratched her tender skin. 'I'll have tea ready in five
minutes,' she assured him hastily.

He didn't answer, but she felt happier that some of
the rage died from his face. If he noticed the bruises on
her body from his less than gentle handling, he didn't
mention them. He merely watched darkly as she picked
up the lemonade bottle and the empty wrappings and
put them in the picnic basket.

'Are you coming straight back to the house or are you going for a walk first?' she asked, remembering his habits.

'I'll walk along the shore while you put the kettle on,' he said grimly, after another moment of regarding her closely. 'I guess a breath of fresh air wouldn't do me any harm.'

By the time he returned she had the tea made and set out on the kitchen table, but he merely picked up his cup and carried it through to his study with a brief word of thanks. Wistfully Paula looked after him. She had hoped he might sit down and have his tea with her. Perhaps she should have kept him longer on the beach? No, she frowned, finishing her own tea and going to shower the sand off her limbs before making a start on dinner. It wouldn't do any good to rush things. This was one time, she sensed, when it might be better to be patient.

She dressed with more care that evening than she'd done recently. She wanted to look attractive for she was suddenly determined not to give Luke up without a fight! She brushed her hair until it shone and used her favourite perfume. She was amazed at how quickly she could make herself presentable now. When she thought of all the time she used to take, she grimaced incredulously.

Greatly daring, she set her place opposite Luke in the dining-room again. He might order her to leave, but she didn't think he would be that offensive. And, even if he didn't speak to her, it would be better than sitting alone in the kitchen.

Luke's eyes were cool as they swept her slender form in the clinging white sundress, but he didn't order her out. After appraising her steadily, with raised brows, he sat down and got on with his soup. She noticed, though, that he didn't attempt to pull out her chair or pour her wine. She was about to ask if she might have some when she changed her mind. It might be more advisable to keep a clear head; a few drinks might find her saying something foolish.

'Have you had a good day?' she asked, when the silence began getting her down. She felt an increasing interest in his work, but he never talked about it.

He didn't appear to be inclined to be more eloquent on the subject now. 'So-so,' he replied.

'Do you type your own manuscripts?' she persevered stubbornly.

'When I'm here,' he shrugged. 'It's easier.'

Whatever did he mean by that? Paula stared at him anxiously for a few seconds, then changed the angle of her questions slightly. 'When you aren't here, where do you live? You never told me.'

'I have an apartment in New York——' Hesitating a moment, he added, 'I travel a lot, though not as much as I used to, mainly seeking local colour. If I need a lot of detailed background, I might stay six months in one place.'

Paula held her breath until she realised he wasn't really telling her anything. He was probably describing the working life of many successful writers.

'I've read a lot of your books,' she smiled, as he glanced up. 'I specially liked the one you did set in Cairo. I felt I was there.'

'Really?'

His tone and impassive expression implied that he had long ago lost all interest in such naïve remarks. Paula met his steely grey eyes, her smile fading. 'Anyway, I thought it was good.'

His nod of apparent appreciation did nothing to prepare her for the shock of the question that followed. 'How long were you engaged to Ian Doobray?' he asked conversationally.

# CHAPTER EIGHT

WAS Luke punishing her for asking too many questions? Paula let out the breath she was holding painfully. It seemed fairly obvious that he considered she was getting far too personal and was retaliating. She hadn't been asking about his life out of mere curiosity; she was really interested, but this was something he didn't understand. As things had been between them, perhaps his attitude wasn't to be wondered at, but surely he realised people could change?

As for Ian—carefully Paula laid down her fork, avoiding Luke's piercing glance. Luke had caught her off guard. She had no wish to hide what had been between Ian and herself, it had been little enough, but how could she explain how empty her engagement had been without condemning herself further in Luke's eyes? She decided to be brief, hoping this would satisfy him. 'A few months.'

It didn't. Luke pressed on, as if he had a whole string of questions lined up. 'You enjoyed a long engagement?'

Ian hadn't. He had wanted to get married immediately she had accepted his proposal, she had been the one to hold back. Strangely, she found herself answering Luke more or less as she had answered Ian. 'I didn't feel there was any need to hurry.'

'What puzzles me——' he began, then stopped. 'Never mind,' he muttered. 'So what happened?'

This time it was easier. 'My status changed,' she said dryly, 'and so did Ian. He decided to call the whole thing off—with the help, I believe, of parental pressure.'

'Didn't you think he was worth fighting for?'

'My pride wouldn't let me,' she admitted. 'I guess I was so angry I didn't think about it.'

131

'Does that mean,' Luke asked tersely, 'you'd have him back?'

'No,' she hesitated only a second. 'I didn't love him. I didn't believe in it, but I've changed my opinion about that since then.'

'Since when?'

The sarcasm in his voice hurt so much she didn't dare risk exposing herself to more by confessing only since last night. He would be openly derisive if she tried to convince him that he was responsible for making her see what kind of person she was, for filling her with regret. She didn't expect him to understand how the discovery of her love for him had changed everything, for she barely understood herself.

'Since I came here, I believe,' she replied cautiously, wondering how much she could say without giving herself completely away. 'I think your island was teaching me new values before I realised it, Luke.' Unevenly she continued, 'W—when you discovered what I was up to, I think the shock made me see myself as I never had before.'

'Spare me,' retorted Luke, with black-browed harshness. 'I'd rather you stayed your bitchy, self-seeking self than try and pretend you've turned over a new leaf. People don't change overnight, Paula, so don't ask me to believe the drivel you're spouting out now!'

Hopelessly she rose to bring in the sweet. It terrified her that anyone could have the power to fill her with such despair. Fearing she might burst into tears, she fled to the kitchen.

To her surprise Luke followed. 'I won't bother with pudding, if you don't mind. I'll just take some coffee into the study.'

'Haven't you done enough for one day?' she asked impulsively, forgetting, as she swung round to face him, that her eyes were bright with tears. 'You look tired.'

His mouth twisted with grim amusement. 'Worrying over me now, are you?' he mocked. 'I must admit you're a trier. I've neglected my work in the past few weeks. It won't do me any harm to put in a few extra hours.'

The evening stretched long and empty when Luke left. After she had washed up, it seemed too fine a night to just sit in the lounge, so she decided to go for a walk along the beach and followed Luke's footsteps to where he had gone earlier. She couldn't match the length of his strides, but she found the imprint of his footsteps in the sand oddly comforting. She was surprised to find it was almost a mile before they turned. He must have been walking at a furious pace, because he had been gone no more than twenty minutes.

Sitting down on a flat rock, Paula brushed back her red-gold curls and gazed about her. Everywhere was beauty, peace and calm. As she breathed it in, it soothed the ache in her heart until she was smiling softly. It was strange, she mused, that just as she had fallen in love with Luke, she had began to feel an affinity for his island. For days, now, she had enjoyed exploring it. She wasn't sure when it had stopped feeling like a prison, but it had. Now she knew she could stay here for weeks without being bored. She could even live here if she had to, with Luke and a few books and records for company, when he was busy. Most of the time she would enjoy being busy herself, looking after him and their children. Abruptly she halted such foolish thoughts, digging tense toes against the rock on which she was sitting. What on earth was she thinking about, thinking such things! She had no excuse for letting her thoughts run away with her.

It was after ten when she returned, and there was still no sign of Luke. Realising what time it was, she wondered why he hadn't been to see if she was trying to escape again. He must believe she wouldn't, after making sure she belonged to him. An hour later, she went slowly to bed. Going upstairs, she glanced in the direction of his study, but there was no sound. Was she shameless, she frowned, for hoping he would join her?

She wanted him so badly, she didn't care whether it was right or wrong. That she loved him seemed all that was important.

Feeling restless, she indulged in a leisurely bath, slipping on her pure silk satin robe before leaving the bathroom. She hadn't been going to seek Luke out, but when she saw him crossing the upper hall towards her, on his way to his own bedroom, she couldn't help pausing.

Her heart thumping with a kind of tremulous anticipation, she waited for him, feeling strangely breathless. The twilight had faded to a deep grey, so she couldn't see the expression in his eyes as he caught sight of her, but after last night, surely she had the right to expect him at least to be friendly? He might not have been over-friendly at dinner, but last night he had made love to her so passionately it didn't seem possible that he could just walk away and forget it.

Her stomach tightened as he approached, then walked straight past her, with such an air of indifference she flinched. 'Luke?' she entreated, a note of desperation in her voice.

He halted, then turned slowly, his face impassive. Paula's whole body wrenched with the pain of the total rejection she found there. As his eyes broodingly searched her face, she didn't attempt to conceal her confusion or love. Had her surrender, humiliation and loss of pride, meant nothing more to him than the fleeting triumph of revenge? He had taken her in a blaze of anger, appeasing a physical hunger, but surely, underneath he had been motivated by more than just that? Yet, as he stared at her dispassionately, doubts and fears began to attack her already wavering confidence.

'Yes?' he prompted coldly.

Her gaze fell from his face, unable to sustain the challenging glint in the dark eyes. He was clearly asking what she wanted. How could she say she wanted him and not appear wanton? Her palms began to sweat and she rubbed them together. 'I wondered if you were still angry with me,' she murmured.

'Paula!' he said grimly, his eyes going slowly over her while his mouth twisted derisively, 'isn't there an ounce of self-respect in your whole body? You drove me, last night, to taking you in anger. Now you're somehow trying to turn the fact that I found you desirable to your own advantage. What more can you hope to achieve?'

Paula felt herself growing white and she wished she had the strength of mind to move away, but the powerful sexual chemistry between them was holding her immobile. Luke was watching her silently, and, as his eyes narrowed suddenly, he slowly released a few buttons on his shirt. It was the unconscious action of a man on his way to bed, but Paula sensed he was using it now to punish her further.

'You're wrong, Luke,' she said unsteadily, averting her eyes from his bared chest. 'I don't want anything more from you except your trust and respect, but I know I'll have to deserve such things before you give them. Meanwhile,' she faltered, 'because I deliberately set out to deceive you, I'm willing to offer anything as compensation.'

'Now you're trying to set yourself up as a kind of sacrificial angel,' he mocked.

That wasn't the impression she had hoped to give, but she knew she had expressed herself badly. She wished she could have explained exactly how she felt, but it was difficult to lay one's soul bare without some encouragement. 'I'm certainly no angel, Luke,' she attempted to joke, 'as you should know!'

'You seemed one, last night,' he muttered with sudden hoarseness. 'You say you'd be willing to give me anything, but you've already given—or did I take?—an awful lot.'

He reached out lightly to touch her silken hair, and involuntarily her eyes widened. 'I need you,' she whispered, before she could stop herself. 'I don't know what's happening to me, but it's like a fire inside me, eating me up. I was wrong when I said I didn't want you. I can't seem to stop myself.'

'Paula!' he groaned, as the dam holding back her self-control burst, propelling her into his arms. She put her own arms round him, holding him tightly.

'Oh, Paula!' he muttered against her throat.

She gasped as his tongue and mouth traced her collarbone, as her robe fell apart. 'Do you know what you're doing?' he rasped.

She didn't answer. It was sufficient that he was carrying her into her bedroom after picking her up in his powerful arms. Something crackled in the air between them, making her lips tingle even before they parted to receive his kiss. Their clothes were torn from their limbs by Luke's impatient hands as they fell on the bed together, and Paula's face flushed as she was made fully aware of his arousal. Their bodies melded in a fusion of white-hot shattering delight. Her breasts pressed against his chest, her thighs to his, and she gasped as she became aware of the steely strength of him against her soft, slender form.

'I want you,' he said thickly, his hands beginning a slow exploration of her sensitive breasts while his tongue encircled each swollen nipple until she was writhing beneath him from the feeling he sent coursing to every inch of her body.

Half-consciously she sensed he was trying to slow down, but they were both trembling with urgent need when his hands wandered lower, towards the smooth region of her inner thighs. She was aching with desire for him and not trying to hide it as she felt him enter her. Then her soft cry of pleasure was stilled against his mouth as his long length stretched over her and he took her completely into his arms. His hot mouth filled her with desperate passion and she responded without reservation. She let reason drown in a tide of rising pleasure as they crested the waves in perfect and absolute unison together, until everything exploded in a peak of feeling far greater than even that which Paula had experienced the night before. She gave herself up to it completely, and Luke's moan of gratification was evidence that he had shared her feelings of intense satisfaction.

As had happened the previous morning, Luke wasn't with her when she woke up, but it didn't bother her nearly as much as it had done before. Today she was certain he cared for her and she felt incredibly happy.

When she eventually dressed and went to find him, she was startled to discover that it was almost eleven. She had slept in again. She must ask Luke to wake her in the mornings when he got up. She flushed on realising what such thoughts implied, but not unhappily. She saw long, idyllic days ahead and even more wonderful nights spent in his arms. She didn't intend interfering with his work. While she got on with the cooking and housework, he could write in peace in his study. A tremulous smile curved her warm pink lips as she thought how changed her life was going to be from now on. The cold past was gone whatever the future held, she would never dwell on what had been again. She would remember her parents, but with love, instead of the resentment that had consumed her since they died.

Quickly she rubbed the sudden tears from her eyes. If Luke caught her crying he would think she was miserable, and this was the last impression she wanted to give. Grabbing a duster, she went back upstairs to make the beds—and blushed as she remembered there would be only one to make this morning.

She had believed Luke to be in his study and didn't go to speak to him for fear of interrupting a vital train of thought. His coffee cup had been rinsed out on the sink, along with a plate, which suggested he had made his own breakfast. Instead of bothering him with more coffee, which he might not want, Paula decided to make an early and substantial lunch.

She was finishing off the lounge when she was sure

she heard voices, and going to the window, she gazed in consternation at the sight of Luke coming up the track with Monica Frank and two other people in tow. He was helping Monica along and she was laughing up into his face as she clung to his arm while the couple behind them joined in her amusement at something Luke was saying. He and the other man were each carrying a suitcase, Paula felt her spirits plummet as she realised this could only mean one thing. Luke had visitors, and they were staying!

'I don't believe it!' Paula heard herself whispering in an anguished voice. Luke wouldn't—he couldn't! Frantically she clutched her arms around her, as if trying to ward off threatening hurt. He hadn't mentioned anyone coming to stay, he had always maintained he had no time for visitors. Yet here was Monica Frank arriving, looking very sure of her welcome, as though it had all been arranged.

Paula was so stunned that she hadn't a chance to remove the cotton scarf she had tied round her hair or get rid of her duster before the party was upon her. They swept into the lounge in a gale of loud talk and laughter. Luke appeared to be enjoying himself immensely.

'Ah, here's Paula!' he grinned expansively. 'I told you you wouldn't have to look after yourself, my dear,' this to Monica. 'When Rose had to rush off, Paula was at a loose end—too many models chasing too few jobs, you know, so instead of returning to London, she kindly offered to step into Rose's shoes, so to speak.'

While Paula did her best to swallow a gasp, Monica frowned, then said suspiciously, 'Models don't usually housekeep, darling.'

'This one does.' Luke glanced at Paula—she thought warningly. 'Beggars cannot be choosers; that goes for both of us. I'm right in the middle of my next book and Alvin's tearing his hair out for the last act of my latest play. I hadn't time to start advertising for someone willing to cook and scrub for me here.'

'How long is she hired for?' asked Monica doubtfully, as if Paula wasn't there.

'Another month, provisionally,' Luke replied slowly.

Bewilderment and indignation were still swamping Paula's voice when Monica muttered grudgingly, 'As you say, I suppose it's Hobson's choice. Just so long as you don't expect me to help out, or take over if she happens to get fed-up. Cilla isn't domesticated either, are you, darling?' She turned to the other woman, who vaguely shook her head, while her husband strolled to the window to admire the view.

This can't be happening! Paula thought desperately. Why is Luke doing this to me? There must be some explanation! She saw several, none of which she liked, but for the moment she felt helpless to protest. However, when Luke said coolly, 'Perhaps we could have coffee, Paula, before you start lunch?' she looked at him squarely and asked, 'Would it be possible to have a word with you, Luke? Just about supplies.'

'Of course,' he agreed blandly, following her out, after telling the others to make themselves at home and he'd be back in a minute.

In the kitchen, he closed the door carefully. 'Now what's bothering you?' he asked curtly.

Paula found it difficult to speak coolly when he stared at her as if she were a stranger, instead of the girl he had held in his arms all night. 'Why have you brought Miss Frank here, Luke?' she asked. She tried not to sound resentful, realising she was in no position to make demands.

He eyed her narrowly, so she couldn't see what lay in his eyes. She knew she must look pale, possibly haggard, but she was still trembling from a kind of underlying shock. Luke clearly didn't appreciate being questioned; he wouldn't be used to being accountable to anyone.

Paula realised she might be jumping to the wrong conclusions, but she couldn't stop herself from pressing for an answer.

'Luke?' she entreated.

'Monica was once in a play of mine,' he replied, at last. 'She might be in another.'

Paula gulped and tried another tack. 'I thought you didn't encourage people to come here?'

'Monica is also a friend of mine,' he said sharply.

Paula went cold, a shiver running through her. 'You told her I was the housekeeper.'

'Temporarily.'

'Luke,' she implored unevenly, 'you surely don't expect me to cook and scrub for your guests? You said I was to look after you and I agreed, but you didn't say anything about anyone else.'

'Have you any objection?' he demanded harshly. 'You don't imagine you've had time yet to work off your debt?'

Paula swallowed something hurting in her throat, her green eyes dark with pain. So making love to her had just been part of what he considered she owed him! Bitterly she clenched her hands in an effort to cope with the feeling of sickness sweeping over her. 'No,' she agreed, 'but I thought it was just between you and me.'

'And don't you think,' he observed reasonably, 'it would be better kept that way? Monica accepts that you're here as my housekeeper. In a modern world, girls from different backgrounds are doing all kinds of things, especially in places like the Caribbean. Today you're as likely to find the daughter of an earl installed as a domestic as the type of girl who did such work a century ago.'

Why did she feel he wasn't concentrating on what he was saying? 'I don't see what that has to do with me,' she frowned. 'Why don't you just let me go, Luke? There seems no sense in carrying on as we're doing, and I'm sure you and Miss Frank would rather be alone.'

What she was suggesting was something he must know she dared not put in words, that having her here could only be embarrassing after he had slept with her, now that Monica had caught up with him.

'You aren't going anywhere until ...' he paused abruptly, his teeth clamping in mid-sentence in such a way as to make Paula wonder what he had been going to say. Her widening eyes were clearly curious, but he only snapped, 'Until I say so. And that won't be for a while yet.'

'You won't change your mind?'

'No,' he refused impatiently. 'It's convenient to have someone capable of looking after my guests while I'm busy.'

'If you insist,' she said, giving in dully.

'If you look at it from your own point of view,' he bit out tersely, 'you'll see that leaving in a hurry might achieve nothing but a lot of gossip that could even follow you across the Atlantic.'

'I'm not bothered about gossip any more,' she replied, lowering her eyes so he shouldn't see the hurt in them. 'But you're quite right, otherwise. I must still owe you, so I'll look after your guests to the best of my ability.'

Her meek tones obviously made him suspicious, because he said grimly, after a long stare, 'No tricks!'

'I've had two weeks' practice. I'm actually getting to like keeping house,' she returned bleakly.

'But not permanently addicted,' he taunted, 'or you wouldn't be so keen to leave.'

His eyes raked her so closely, she felt confused. 'You have Monica, Luke. I realise she means a lot to you or you wouldn't have her here. Perhaps I'm afraid I might say something embarrassing.'

'Feel free,' he shrugged.

What he meant was that both Monica and he were too sophisticated to let a little thing like his taking another woman to bed bother them. Monica, if confronted with such a thing, would simply believe that Luke had been making use of the nearest available female to satisfy a normal masculine urge. Luke might indulge himself with all the women he liked, as long as Monica became the permanent one in his life. Paula wasn't that slow that she hadn't absorbed the message in the other girl's eyes!

'What good would it do me if I did?' she sighed. 'I think I'd be better employed trying to improve my cooking than trying to be bitchy to your girl-friend.'

'Your cooking's beginning to get pretty good,' he praised, without denying that Monica was his girl-friend, as she had hoped he might. 'You said you wanted to speak to me about supplies, or was that only an excuse?'

'An excuse.'

His eyes softened at the dejection she failed to hide and he didn't rebuke her. 'Let me know if we're running short of anything.'

'Will do.'

'Fine, I'll leave you to it, then,' his voice hardened again at the careless tone it had cost her a lot to achieve. 'But stop sulking, there's a good girl. Monica doesn't care for glum faces.'

Did he have to be so deliberately cruel! That she resisted an inclination to throw the coffee pot after him must be a sign she had grown up. Wasn't he aware that the only face Monica would tolerate around was her own? However, seeing how good cooks—cooks of any kind—weren't easy to come by on islands like this, Monica might think twice before unsheathing her claws. While she pretended to adore Luke, she might be hard put to it to sustain such a fallacy should she have to do all the work herself.

Trying not to care too much, Paula prepared coffee and biscuits which she loaded on a tray and carried through to the lounge. She was about to beat a hasty retreat when Monica said quickly, 'After Luke has shown me to my room, I'd like you to unpack for me. Luke will tell you when I'm ready for you, won't you, darling?'

Paula flushed a deep pink on being reminded so sharply of her own high-handed attitude with Rose when she had first arrived. She tried to ignore the subtle hint in Monica's voice that Luke could be delayed in her room for some time.

'Of course,' she muttered.

Luke shocked her by offering humorously, 'I can unpack for you, Monica—that is if you don't mind your things just being tipped into a few drawers. Paula has enough to do and we have to talk. I'm sure you wouldn't want her interrupting us.'

Monica was smiling smugly as Paula retreated to the kitchen again. How could he? she wondered miserably. After making passionate love to her on the two previous nights, he was turning without regret to someone else. He hadn't pretended to be in love with her, of course. Looking back, she could see how he had possessed her with force and purpose but without love. Luke had been motivated by a prevailing desire for revenge, not because of any softer feelings he might have had for her.

A tear trickled down Paula's cheek, but she felt no anger, her misery was too great. The unhappiness inside her kept all other emotion at bay. The most she could expect from Luke was his reluctant approbation, if she made a good job of looking after Monica. Otherwise he would ignore her, as though she wasn't there.

With a weary sigh she attempted to look at the whole thing objectively. After what she had tried to do to Luke, she supposed she was lucky that he was giving her another chance to prove that the vain and frivolous creature she had been until recently had gone forever. Perhaps she needed to prove to herself, too, that the change she felt in herself was genuine, not just a flash in the pan. If she felt a desire to lead a more meaningful life, shouldn't she be fairly certain that the change in her was going to last?

Nevertheless, despite her new resolutions, it wasn't easy to watch Luke concentrating almost wholly on Monica. Monica, Paula discovered, was adept at sharp little digs. Though she seldom indulged in them when Luke was around, she took a delight in taunting Paula for failing as a model, as well as other things.

'I thought you hadn't got what it takes.' She

surprised Paula, one day, by wandering arrogantly into the kitchen while she was preparing a flan for lunch. When Paula looked up sharply, Monica smiled with her mouth but not her eyes. 'After I met you on Barbados, I said to the friends I was with then that you'd never make the grade, and wasn't I right?' Without waiting for Paula to comment, she smiled on, 'Being an actress gives one insight into people's characters, you know, perhaps through having to throw oneself into so many different roles?'

Wishing she would throw herself over a cliff, Paula sighed. She could recognise Monica's type a mile off, and she had never been an actress! 'I quite like what I'm doing now,' she replied, as politely as she could. 'Cooking is interesting.'

'Do cooks usually wear shorts?' Monica enquired, eyeing the perfection of Paula's long slender legs disapprovingly.

'It depends,' Paula retorted, in what she hoped was a calm voice. 'Cooking in this climate calls for something cool, and shorts are about all I've got.'

Monica's beauty was spoiled by a thinning mouth. 'You're an opportunist, I believe, but the next time you think of changing your career, I should look before you leap. Obviously,' she picked up the flan with patronising fingers, 'in coming here, you expected to be cooking other things. What a shame I put a stop to your little game by arriving as I did!'

Paula felt her temper, which she had thought gone for good, rising. Swiftly she controlled it again. Monica was overdoing the clichés and being downright rude, but what purpose would it serve if she retaliated and they flew at each other's throats?

Shrugging, she asked abruptly, while retrieving her flan, 'What made you decide to come here?'

'Luke asked me, my dear,' returned Monica smugly. 'He sounded desperate enough to beg.'

'Beg?'

'Don't look so startled,' Monica preened. 'He wants

to write a part exactly for me, and he thought the best way to do that was for us to get together. Naturally, as we're old friends, I've stayed with him before.'

Turning away, Paula felt suddenly ill. So Luke had invited Monica to Sabina—after spending the night with her! He must have decided, because she hadn't been able to hide her increasing response to his lovemaking, that it wansn't punishment enough. He must have planned in cold blood that she should be really hurt, this time, by bringing Monica here and flaunting her before her. Paula felt as wounded as though he had pierced her with a dagger through the heart. Savagely she began rinsing the vegetables she was preparing for the salad, hoping Monica would take the hint and go.

Monica, however, wasn't finished with her yet. As Paula turned her back on her, she said sweetly, 'I'd like my room done out again, as soon as you can. I realise you've done it once this morning, but Luke came in while I was trying to find my suntan lotion and he trailed sand all over the place.'

'I'll do it as soon as I've a minute,' Paula replied, glancing over her shoulder, straight into Luke's eyes.

'Just came to see how long lunch will be.' His glance flickered warily from one girl to the other. 'Hello, Monica,' he said, before Paula could reply, 'I'm sorry if I've been neglecting you today, but I've been rather busy. I think I've worked up quite an appetite—that's why I came to see if lunch was ready.'

Monica sidled up to him, kissing his cheek lightly. 'I knew you'd be hungry, darling—that's why I came to hurry Paula up. I guess the morning's activities have made us both hungry.'

Luke put an arm round her while watching Paula mockingly. 'Seems like our cook has lost her tongue!'

'The soup's ready to bring in,' Paula told him, her face pale.

'It's too hot for soup!' complained Monica.

'This is chilled.'

'Chilled soup can be horrible.'

Paula thought of adding poison to Monica's. It would serve her right! It made her bitter to realise how much she envied the other girl the arm she had round her.

Luke spoke soothingly to Monica, shielding her from Paula's stony-eyed gaze. 'Bob has a drink waiting for you in the lounge, honey. You'd better go and get it before he brings it in here. Then you never know when we might get to eat.'

Monica nodded, trying to look reluctant, which she never could be with a drink in the offing. It was really pathetic just how transparent Monica was, when she wasn't on her guard, Paula thought dryly.

Paula swallowed, once she was alone with Luke. Her gaze focused itself on the second top button of his shirt, rather than lift higher to his eyes. Just the same, she was conscious of his hard jaw and strong chin, somewhere level near her forehead. The clean, male fragrance of his aftershave dominated her sense of smell and disturbed her breathing. When he addressed her, she found herself watching the movement of the chiselled contours of his mouth with the same hunger he was professing for his lunch.

'Don't rub Monica up the wrong way,' he was saying, 'I don't like it and neither does she.'

'I don't mean to,' she replied uneasily, wondering what was coming next. Didn't Luke realise what he was doing to her? How much she longed for him.

Unexpectedly he put a hand under her chin, forcing her to look at him. Something flashed between them as their eyes met, sending enchanting sparks through her veins, making her blood surge to a fever pitch of desire. Her heart began to throb as his gaze smouldered and held hers. For a taut moment she thought he was going to kiss her, because his breathing deepened, but he merely thrust her away.

'Monica isn't always easy to get on with,' he drawled, his face once more an impersonal mask. 'It's her artistic temperament. One has to make allowances.'

'I understand.'

He frowned at her meek voice and lowered eyes. 'You sounded irritable when I came in. Had Monica said something to upset you?'

'Nothing more than usual.'

His mouth tightened. 'Isn't it more a case of all work and no play getting you down and Monica being handy to use as a scapegoat?'

Stung by his caustic remark, Paula retorted, 'I don't take my troubles out on other people.'

'Wouldn't it be better if you tried to get along with her?' he suggested curtly.

'How long will she be staying?' asked Paula bleakly.

'As long as it takes,' he parried grimly. 'You don't need to keep asking—you'll know soon enough.'

That must be until he and Monica had reached some sort of agreement. Her heart went cold. Until he persuaded Monica to marry him, perhaps? Paula knew she might never survive such an announcement. She hoped she would be gone long before then.

She watched him leaving the kitchen with dull eyes. 'I'll begin serving lunch right away,' she called after him.

Paula didn't eat her meals in the dining-room, she had retired to the kitchen again. Luke hadn't argued this time, either, and she was relieved. It meant not having to sit through an interminable hour hearing him laughing and talking with everyone but herself.

Cilla and Bob Drake, Monica's two friends, were a curious couple. Bob's parents, Paula gathered, had left enough money to keep him comfortably without working. Most of his days were spent on a lounger in the garden with his wife usually beside him. Cilla had let drop, one day, that while Monica was still in her thirties, both she and Bob were almost fifty. Paula had a feeling that Luke didn't like Bob Drake all that much, which she didn't consider so surprising as they were completely different types. That was why she believed he was really serious about Monica. If he hadn't been, it was doubtful that he would have tolerated having people here with whom he had nothing in common, even though they were her friends.

Paula took extra care over dinner, that evening, having found some recipes in a magazine to try out. She did the salmon mousse after lunch and put it to set in the fridge so she could concentrate on the stuffed fillet of beef and lemon pudding later. Fortunately everything turned out well, but Paula wondered if it would have mattered if she'd had one of her occasional disasters. Monica and her friends seemed more interested in what they were drinking than what they were eating. Certainly they didn't bother to compliment the chef.

Luke did, though. He came to the kitchen, while she was busy washing up and congratulated her himself. 'The beef was especially good,' he said, then hesitated. 'I don't want to hurt your feelings, but was there something missing? I've been going mad trying to think what it could be.'

Paula grinned, grateful that he hadn't mentioned it before the others. 'I've run out of black pepper.'

'Ah,' he laughed, 'why didn't I guess? Do you know, I've thought of nothing else since dinner. Let me know if you're short of other things—I'll have to pop over to the mainland one of these days, so make a list.'

She nodded, then swallowed. When he mentioned going to Barbados, there was something she wanted to ask him, if only she could find the courage.

# CHAPTER NINE

'LUKE,' she pleaded quietly, keeping her eyes on the sink, 'when you do go to Barbados, couldn't I come with you? I realise I haven't paid off my debts yet, but I don't think there's much sense in my staying here any longer.'

'What is it, cold feet?' he countered shortly, coming nearer, so she could feel his eyes fastened on her averted profile.

'Probably,' she admitted, carefully re-rinsing a dish.

To her consternation, he lifted some curls so he could see her face better. 'You're very pale this evening,' he growled. 'Are you feeling all right?'

From time to time he concerned himself over her health, but she didn't imagine it had anything to do with her personally. He was enjoying having guests, so long as he had someone to look after them.

'I'm not on the point of collapse, if that's what you mean,' she replied lightly.

Luke's breathing roughened suddenly as he stared at her. 'You're thinner than you were when you first came, though. Are you eating properly?'

'You think a hearty appetite guards against everything?'

She couldn't see Luke's frown, but she sensed it furrowing his brow as he worked that out. She wanted to cry out in painful frustration that he was so near and yet so distant. Her cheeks flushed with the effort of trying not to look at him and her pulse quickened at the way she could feel him suddenly looking at her. He was running his gaze over her red-gold curls and bent head, and, amazingly, she felt him tremble.

'Paula——' he began, when Bob Drake walked into the kitchen.

'Ah, Luke,' he said, 'we wondered where you'd got

to. Monica wants another drink and she seems to think you're the only one who can mix her one just as she likes it.'

Luke nodded and turned, then halted suspiciously as the other man's eyes went straight to Paula and lingered. 'A model, were you, my dear?' asked Bob eagerly.

Because Bob had been here for days and taken little notice of her, Paula wondered why he was regarding her now as if he hadn't seen her before. Was it because Luke and she had been standing so close together? Uneasily she backed further away from Luke, feeling the tension in her body slacken slightly as her breathing returned to normal with the extra distance between them.

'I haven't done a great deal of modelling,' she shrugged evasively.

'I'd be interested to hear about it, all the same,' Bob smiled. 'And there's no time like the present.'

Paula was relieved when Luke moved nearer again. Bob looked like a man who had just seen untold possibilities unfolding before him.

'Paula's too tired to discuss anything tonight,' Luke said curtly. 'You'd better come with me, Bob, out of the way of temptation.'

Bob moderated a peevish disappointment with a suggestive leer. 'I'd better do as I'm told for now, Paula, but Luke spends a lot of time in his study.'

Did he? Paula was more interested in this piece of information than she was in Bob's over-obvious intentions. She had thought Luke spent most of his time with Monica. He had taken her sailing the other afternoon, and they hadn't returned until late.

Luke, steering Bob firmly from the kitchen, threw her a glance that was taut with disapproval, and Paula's eyes flickered incredulously. He didn't think she was encouraging Bob Drake, did he? Bob must be fifty, if he was a day, and he didn't appeal to her, anyway.

On finishing her duties, Paula felt restless, and

though it was after ten she decided to go for a walk. Talking to Luke had unsettled her, if she went straight to bed she wouldn't sleep. As she left the house, the sound of music followed her to the lounge, along with the shrill sound of Monica's laughter.

Lifting her face to the warm scented night air, Paula wandered by the sea. The waves breaking softly on the shore soothed her, eventually bringing calm to the turmoil of her mind. With each passing day it became more difficult to retain a sense of tranquillity, and she felt grateful for it now. It was midnight when she returned to the house.

There was a light in the window of the room where the Drakes slept. She didn't know whether the others were in bed as well, but there was no noise coming from the lounge, so she thought they might be. She went quietly upstairs so as not to disturb anyone. At the corner of the corridor leading from the top of the staircase, she came to an abrupt halt, only just in time to prevent Luke from seeing her as he carried Monica into her bedroom. Monica's arms were tightly around his neck and Paula could hear her giggling softly as the door closed sharply behind them.

Shocked to the core, Paula was trembling badly even as she stumbled blindly to her own bedroom. Once there, she stood with her back to the door, gulping great breaths of air, as if it had all been knocked out of her. If she had been hit by lightning she didn't think she could have felt worse. Numbly she staggered to the bed, flinging herself across it. Not until then did the hot tears come, tears she had been holding back ever since Luke had brought Monica to Sabina.

Luke had brought Monica here and was sleeping with her. Hadn't he supplied undeniable proof? And what better proof could anyone have than the evidence of their own eyes? Paula groaned aloud into her damp pillow. She had loved Luke, she still loved him; despite everything her love for him refused to die. Miserably she wished it would, so she wouldn't have to bear the pain. As she lay in the darkness, a terrible numbness closed around her heart as she contemplated a future which seemed empty and desolate.

The following morning she felt terrible, and it took a long time under the shower to remove the signs of tears and a restless night from her face. Luke was in the kitchen when she eventually got there. She felt his eyes on her from the moment she walked in, but she couldn't look at him. It was just after six, no one else was about, and as usual the air between them crackled with tension.

'You look tired,' he frowned.

'I wish you'd stop pretending to be worried about me,' she retorted mutinously, her hand shaking as she poured herself some coffee.

'Why don't you go back to bed?' he suggested, as if she had never spoken.

'What's the point?' Still without looking at him, she began unwrapping sliced bread for toast.

'I can get my own breakfast for once,' he said impatiently.

Did he want her out of the way, so she wouldn't see him perhaps taking Monica something? 'There are others besides you,' she snapped, her head was so bad.

'It wouldn't do them any harm, either,' he retorted surprisingly.

'Luke! Will you please shut up and leave me to get on with things,' Paula exclaimed tersely. 'I have my mornings planned, right down to the last minute. And it takes every minute,' she muttered ruefully.

He didn't appear to be listening. He was more absorbed, she suddenly realised, with her face and figure. She had lingered in the shower so long, she hadn't taken much care over dressing. Her shorts were carelessly belted to her narrow waist, her thin shirt, as carelessly buttoned, revealed the creamy cleavage between her full breasts. Yet, though her face was bare of make-up, he seemed to find something about her riveting, for his eyes remained on her and darkened.

'Luke?' she whispered, forgetting Monica, forgetting everything but the almost tangible sensation of something warm and seductive closing in on them.

Abruptly he turned from her, his mouth tightening harshly, and she realised with a shock that he was trying to control his rage. 'You'd better start learning to dress properly,' he snapped, 'unless you want Bob making a nuisance of himself.'

'I think I'm quite capable of coping with Bob.' She hugged her arms about herself protectively.

'Like you did Ron Davis?'

Paula flinched at the hint that she had given Ron encouragement. 'You should know better than to believe that.'

Luke stared down on her, his jaw hard, then he ran a weary hand around the back of his neck. 'I guess you aren't the only one feeling tired this morning.'

Was this an apology? She doubted it. As she looked into his face, some tiredness was evident but she saw mostly indifference. 'Try sleeping in your own bed for a change,' she advised shortly.

A dull colour crept under his skin. 'How the hell do you know where I sleep?'

'It doesn't matter,' she muttered flatly. 'I shouldn't have said that. I realise you're in love with Monica.'

He glared at her pink cheeks. 'You're still talking in riddles.'

But not ones he didn't understand, she thought wearily, knowing it would be impossible to put in words what she had seen last night. 'Maybe I'm jealous,' she hedged, not untruthfully.

His eyes glinted with derision. 'Once you're back to civilisation there'll be plenty of men to help take your mind off me. You'll soon forget what happened here.'

Paula bit her lip at the hardness of his voice. So much for her forlorn hope that he might be willing to forgive her! 'I don't think I'll ever be able to forget,' she whispered.

'I think I'm in a better position to judge,' he rapped,

his voice repressive as he turned suddenly and strode from the kitchen.

Paula watched him go and was glad he hadn't slammed the door when she heard the door of his study open and close. He hadn't gone to Monica, and she felt a rush of relief that was absurd. That he hadn't gone to Monica now didn't alter the fact that he had spent the night with her though. No amount of relief could alleviate the heartache of that.

She had intended going for a quick swim after breakfast, but her headache became so bad she had to go to her room instead. The cramping pains in her stomach and the pounding in her head soon disclosed the reason for her malaise. When Monica looked in and found her prostrate on the bed, she was able to tell her. While not expecting sympathy, she did at least think Monica would keep quiet about it. She was embarrassed, as Monica left, to hear Luke's deep voice outside her door enquiring what was wrong, and Monica replying mockingly that it was just nature bestowing its monthly benevolence.

She felt guilty over considering Monica treacherous when a few minutes later she heard the rattle of crockery by her bedside. To her surprise, on opening her eyes, she discovered it wasn't Monica but Luke, with some tea.

'Oh!' she exclaimed, too dazed to do more than gaze at him. 'You shouldn't have bothered.'

'No trouble,' he said briefly, unscrewing a bottle of aspirin. 'You won't have had any of these?'

'I haven't any.'

'Take them,' he ordered, shaking two tablets from the bottle, his eyes on her flushed, feverish face. 'It's the least a man can do, considering what women have to put up with.'

Uncertainly, she stretched out a hand, then winced as her head threatened to explode as she moved. 'I'll be fine in an hour or two,' she muttered.

Luke waited until the aspirin was down and she had

drunk half the tea. 'Don't worry about lunch,' he said, 'I'll see to it. And,' he threatened, 'you'd better take my advice this time, or else ...'

Paula fell asleep after he had gone and it was late afternoon when she woke. Her head had stopped pounding and she didn't feel so churned up. She lay remembering and marvelling at Luke's kindness. The aspirin had soothed her and she had slept, which must have been just what she needed. Resolutely she swung her feet to the floor, clamping down on a lot of 'if onlys'. Luke was interested in Monica—maybe only temporarily, but if she wasn't permanent there would be others. There was no place for Paula Edison in his life.

She found a note by her bedside along with a jug of water with ice floating in it. It must have been put there recently, because the ice hadn't melted. A frown creased Paula's forehead as she stared at it. Monica wouldn't have brought it, neither would her friend. Cilla wasn't unkind, she was just a negative shadow, although possessive of her husband—which also ruled Bob out. Luke must be responsible, for both the water and the note. She opened the note apprehensively.

'Don't get up,' it read, 'before you're recovered. When you are, I'd like to see you in my study. Cilla is cooking dinner for eight o'clock. Luke.'

So it had been him. Paula's cheeks grew hot as she wondered how much of her had been uncovered when he came in. Her head had driven her to distraction. After he left she had just flung off her clothing and crawled under a sheet. The same sheet was around her waist when she woke up, and she wondered how much he had seen.

Seven found her knocking on the door of his study and obeying his command to come in.

'How are you?' He was working at his desk but rose to get a chair for her. He looked hard at her when she replied that she was feeling better.

'Thanks for the water,' she smiled. 'I drank all of it. I woke up hot and thirsty, and you've no idea how good it tasted!'

'You're sure you're all right?'

'I would have been quite able to cook dinner,' she reproached. 'It wasn't necessary to give my job to Cilla.'

He gave her a curious look and she wished she hadn't sounded so indignant. Lest he read too much into the remark, she said proudly, 'I don't believe in opting out of my obligations. I'll begin again tomorrow.'

Sitting on the edge of his desk, Luke towered above her. 'Tomorrow,' he said carefully, keeping his eyes on her face, 'I'm flying to New York. I can't keep on ignoring the urgent messages I'm getting from my publisher, and there's other business that needs my attention.'

'Oh,' she glanced at him blankly. 'How long will you be gone?'

'I'll be in New York for the next few months.'

Disbelieving, she stared at him. 'I can't go there with you, Luke.'

'Nobody's asking you to,' he said tersely.

'I've grown to love Sabina,' she frowned, 'but I don't think I could stay here by myself that long.'

'You don't understand,' he rasped. 'We're all leaving Sabina tomorrow—you to return to London, while Monica and the Drakes will come with me to New York.'

She squeezed her eyes tightly shut, her body held rigid. Was he playing a game with her? She was already in a highly emotional state and he might have an urge to amuse himself. 'When was this all planned?' she asked, opening her eyes again but not trying to hide the despair in them.

He straightened and paced to the window, oddly restless. 'I thought you'd be delighted,' he said abruptly.

'Yes—Yes, I am,' she exclaimed hurriedly, as he returned to her. 'It's just—unexpected. You kept hinting about keeping me here indefinitely.'

He hesitated, then spoke harshly. 'You acted incomprehensibly, Paula, and I think you deserved all you got. You aren't easy to intimidate and I'm no God that I'm beyond saying things in the heat of the moment, but I never had any intention of keeping you here indefinitely. It wouldn't be practical, for one thing, and I can't take you to New York.'

'You're taking Monica.'

He said thinly, 'She's different.'

Paula's heart plunged at the angry hardness in his voice. She wished she hadn't mentioned Monica. 'Will I ever see you again?' she asked painfully, her face white.

'Unlikely,' he bit out. 'After everything that's happened, do you think I'd want to? Anyway, I guess we'll both be too busy getting on with our lives to have any time to look back. Regret never served a useful purpose, unless it's to teach one never to make the same mistake twice.'

Wondering if he knew how cruel he was being, Paula gazed at him, swamped in misery. A muscle twitched in his jaw, but otherwise his expression was remote. She wanted to whisper that she would never forget, but his hatred was beating the words back like physical blows. She could only stare at him numbly, her eyes burning with unshed tears.

'You'll return to your modelling,' he resumed, 'the kind of life you've been accustomed to. If there are any initial hitches, I'm sure Denis Cranford will be around to help see you through them. You'll be able to lead a fuller life, from now on, seeing how you won't be handicapped by the inhibitions which must have plagued you for so long. You might even welcome your late fiancé into your bed now!'

He had gone too far. Paula's resolve to stay calm crumbled. Her hand flew up with such speed, as she jumped to her feet, he couldn't avoid the stinging slap she bestowed on his cheek. The next second, though, his hand was grasping her wrist in a mind-shattering hold and hauling her against him.

'Don't ever do that again!' His low voice shook with

menace and his glare was too coldly threatening to
ignore. 'I think I once warned you!'

She restrained her free hand with difficulty, her desire
being to flay and scratch as hard as she could. It was a
primitive violence building up inside her, growing out
of control. 'If you must insult me,' she gasped, 'you
can't be surprised if I retaliate!'

'If I've ever insulted you,' he ground out, 'it's never
been without justification. Remember the reason you
came here, Miss Edison? You made a deal to use your
wiles to entice and seduce a man's body and home from
him. That you didn't complete the task wasn't for the
want of trying.'

'You twist everything!'

His hand tightened as she tried to free herself, and he
stared into her eyes for a long moment. 'You're trying
to deny everything.'

'You know I can't,' she gulped. 'You also know that
nothing was quite the way you describe it. If anything
you—you seduced me!'

His narrow eyes ran over her face, taking in the
pleading, defiant eyes, the heavy lashes, the pale skin
now unnaturally flushed. 'You may be able to deceive
yourself, Paula, but that's as far as it goes. If you're
referring to the nights we spent together, you wanted
me every bit as much as I wanted you. There wasn't an
inch of you that wasn't crying out for me.'

'I never admitted that!' she croaked.

'You didn't have to,' the mocking slant to his mouth
confirmed how much he remembered. 'Don't you think
a man can tell?' he taunted. 'I'd never had it so good.
You were like an inextinguishable flame in my arms.
And I don't exaggerate.'

'You must,' she breathed, ashamed to hear him
describing her in the way he was doing. 'I couldn't be
like that, it was a new experience . . .'

'And for me,' he sneered. 'I never dreamed a woman
could be that responsive. You might consider yourself
lucky that I'm letting you go. You'd make an ideal

mistress if I could stomach your deceitfulness.'

Paula's head jerked back in anger. It was painfully obvious that he had no intention of continuing their relationship on any grounds. She had cheated him, but he enjoyed his single state too much to give it up for anyone.

'I don't intend being deceitful any more,' she said hollowly.

For a second something flashed in the depths of his eyes. Briefly she felt a stirring of something very like hope that he did care for her a little. In that moment a surge of such potent longing swept over her that she swayed against him as he released her wrists and he pulled her completely into his arms.

'You don't expect me to believe that?' he jeered.

'I only wish things had been different between us,' she pleaded unhappily.

'So do I,' he replied, his grey eyes taunting, 'but I don't intend doing anything about it. Except perhaps this.'

As he held her closer, Paula was shaken by the power of the desire that raged through her in a relentless tide. No matter how she felt physically, and even when she was furious with him or just plain jealous of Monica's friendship with him, she craved his touch. Lifting anguished eyes, she gazed longingly into the brooding darkness of his.

She was suddenly aware of being crushed against his hard chest and of his hands moving almost tenderly over her. The virility of his tall, powerful body made a shocking impact on all her senses, so compelling she couldn't fight it. She sensed the descent of his mouth with a helpless sigh. It might be the last time he would kiss her, so why deny herself? Feverishly her arms went around him, rediscovering the strong muscles at the back of his neck. Her lips parted willingly under the ruthless onslaught of his as his hungry mouth probed the inner sweetness of hers.

Wildly she tried to satisfy some of her own aching

hunger. How was she to survive the future without him? As his hands caressed her, causing a delicious ripple of sensation to flame through her, she sighed blissfully. She felt the need in him as she pressed against him. His hot intense look was devouring as he dragged his mouth from hers and heat flooded to her face as his head bent to trail moist, warm kisses over her throat.

'Oh, Luke,' she moaned, 'I do love you.'

Burying his face in her hair, he muttered, 'You smell of flowers. Your skin feels like silk. You're in my blood and I have to get you out of it.'

Harshly his lips crushed hers again and dizzily she realised why he was kissing her. It wasn't because he cared for her, he was trying to exorcise her. Yet his skilful caresses melted the sharp revulsion she felt and the urgent insistence of his hands and mouth stoked the flames within her to new heights.

The pressure of his hard body and lengthening kisses did nothing to discourage the wild turmoil of her thoughts. The certain knowledge that he wanted her as much as she wanted him sent fire leaping through her speeding heart-beats. He seemed as inflamed as she was, as he groaned aloud as he claimed her mouth again and again. She felt shivery, yet hot with a radiant emotion. Maybe, she thought dazedly, there was a chance that he might forgive her and learn to love her. Passionately she returned his kisses, until the heat of their fiercely knit bodies became so fierce she thought they might both go up in flames.

'Luke!' Monica had an irritating habit of calling for him when she was a mile off. She alerted the pair locked in each other's arms before she threw back the door and walked in.

'Luke,' she said again, then paused as he let go of Paula and turned, deliberately blocking her from Monica's view until she tidied her shirt.

'What is it?' he asked tersely.

'Merely the matter of your dinner getting cold and Cilla's temper getting hot,' Monica replied sarcastically, doing her best to peer around the width of his shoulders to see what Paula was doing.

'I'll come at once,' he said, but without apology, herding Monica out.

With twin flags of pink in her cheeks, Paula swung to face the wall while her trembling hands fumbled with uncooperative buttons. She jerked as if shot when Luke's voice struck her unsuspecting back.

'Come and get some dinner when you're ready,' he ordered curtly. 'Don't be long.'

At least he showed some concern for her welfare—but he might have shown the same for a dog or cat. Miserably, Paula wiped away a tear. He was shutting her out again, denying the unspoken feelings that existed between them, and tomorrow it would be too late. After tomorrow they would never see each other again. Her heart bleak with churning emotions, she trailed to the kitchen, weighed down by an unhappiness she knew she was going to have to learn to live with.

Next morning she went through the motions of packing her clothes and tidying the house like someone in a dream. After the trauma of the hour she had spent in Luke's study, she was as eager now to leave Sabina as he appeared to be. She felt in such a state of nerves and tension, she feared she might have a breakdown when she returned to London. If she could get that far without betraying the terrible state she was in, she might be lucky.

After seeing to her personal belongings, she made a special effort to deal with the kitchen; for Rose's sake she wanted to leave it as immaculate as she had found it. Taking a last look around, her eyes glazed with tears. She had never reckoned on becoming so fond of the island. Her love for it had grown with her love for Luke, though he held her heart completely.

He found her picking up her suitcase to carry to the boat. The others had already made their way there.

'We're waiting for you,' he said coldly.

He had been assisting his friends and they had only

had to get themselves ready. Neither Monica nor Cilla had lifted a finger after cooking dinner the previous evening. Paula hadn't been able to eat any dinner. She had made herself some tea and toast which she had carried back to her bedroom, but she had found the dinner dishes waiting for her when she got up that morning. When Luke had popped his head around the kitchen door at six, he had frowned when he'd seen what she was doing, but he hadn't offered any sympathy. He had merely stared at her grimly for a long, tense moment before going out again.

As well as having the dinner dishes to wash and pack away, she had had breakfast to prepare and serve. You'd think he would realise! she thought. 'I'm coming,' she answered, walking past him stiffly.

As he secured the door, he called after her sharply, 'You aren't thinking of staying on in Barbados, are you? I forgot the hotel owes you a few days.'

'No,' she kept her face averted. 'Those belong to the Cranfords; you can tell your cousin if you like. If you hadn't been able to book me on an immediate flight, I should have stayed somewhere else until I got one.'

'Good,' he crisped.

'Luke?' Suddenly she turned on the track, glancing up at him with anguished eyes. 'Do you love Monica?'

Swerving to avoid her, he snapped, 'I'd rather not answer that.'

'You sleep with her.'

He refused to be drawn. 'I suggest you stop delaying us with presumptuous questions, Paula. We don't have all day to get to the airport.'

All the way to Barbados, she watched him handling the boat, not caring if the others noticed. She wasn't sure if Luke was aware of her almost constant regard, because he kept his eyes grimly on what he was doing. Monica retired to the cabin, complaining that the heat on deck was giving her a headache. Paula wondered how the other girl could look so dissatisfied with life when she was going to New York with Luke?

At the airport, Paula had only a short wait before her flight number was called. It was still comparatively early when she said goodbye to Luke and his companions. The Drakes were talking of going on to Miami, which meant that Monica would be alone with Luke.

His face was a mask as he wished her a pleasant journey. Never once did he betray the fact that he was going to do anything other than forget her. As her plane left the ground Paula buried her white face in a book, in an attempt to hide the tears that coursed down her cold cheeks.

In London she went straight to her flat. As she let herself in and closed the door behind her, she gazed around with dull eyes. It looked cold and lonely; suddenly she hated it and knew she couldn't remain here. The fridge was empty as she had let no one know she was returning, but she didn't feel hungry. Making herself a cup of black coffee, from a jar of instant she found, she sat down to think.

The whole of the following week she spent sorting out her affairs, something she knew she should have done long ago. To begin with she disposed of the flat. That wasn't difficult, as small properties like hers were greatly in demand and in short supply. The final settling up would take time, and she left the details for her solicitor to deal with, but after the amount still owing on her mortgage was deducted, there was enough left to enable her to rent a modest room in another part of the city.

'Why are you doing this, Paula?' Denis Cranford asked, catching her on the phone, on the day she moved out. 'Why haven't you been to see me, to discuss what went wrong in the Caribbean? I've been worried to death ever since Luke Armstrong spoke to me.'

She could imagine Luke hadn't dealt with him very gently! 'I didn't think there was any point in coming to see you and talking about it,' she said dismissively. 'Luke—Mr Armstrong was too sharp for us. I'll admit he tricked me into betraying myself, but that's all in the game, isn't it? He was understandably annoyed,'—why defend him? 'but he might still sell you the island,'—heaven forbid! 'It needn't deter you that this attempt failed.'

'It seemed to be succeeding.' Denis sounded mystified. 'Did you ever discover exactly where we went wrong?'

'It was probably my fault,' Paula confessed. 'I lacked the necessary expertise.'

'We'll pay you what we arranged, of course,' Denis's voice changed to a purr. 'Perhaps you would have dinner with me?'

'No, thank you,' she refused sharply, well able to guess what Denis had in mind. 'I've changed my mind about any remuneration; I was crazy for agreeing to work for you in the first place, but maybe we've both learned a lesson. And the next time you send someone to do a job like that I'd advise you to choose a girl with more experience.'

She was shaking as she put down the phone while he was still protesting. She had no intention of listening to Denis gabbling apologies he didn't really mean. She just wanted to put the whole episode behind her. If she could forget Luke as well, the future might be easier. What would Denis Cranford have said if she'd told him she intended changing her life-style completely? He liked the idea of escorting a well known model, but would he have been so keen to take her out, she wondered, if she had told him she was thinking of becoming someone's cook?

The day after she moved to her new address, she visited an agency that supplied domestic staff as well as governesses and nannies.

'There isn't a great demand for work of this kind, so there are usually vacancies,' the woman who interviewed her smiled. She offered Paula a choice of three jobs and Paula listened attentively while she described each individually.

'Which one do you think I should apply for?' she asked tentatively. 'They all sound nice.'

The woman studied her thoughtfully. 'You say you've only had a few weeks' actual experience?'

'Yes.' Paula had explained how she had looked after four adults on a Caribbean island. 'I discovered that I'm a very good cook. I'd really like to be a children's nannie, but I've had no training.'

'You like children?'

Paula nodded, rather sadly, knowing that as she couldn't marry Luke, she wouldn't have any of her own.

'If you'd allow me to advise you,' the agent said, with another keen glance, 'why don't you go to the American couple? They only want someone for a month. Then you could consider taking a course in nursery training, which would provide you with the necessary qualifications to do the kind of work you'd really like to do.'

Paula thanked her and promised to think about it. It seemed a very good idea—if she could afford it.

'This American couple,' the agent explained in greater detail, 'are over here on business and entertain a lot. Mrs Martin thought she could manage herself, but she's finding it difficult. As well as a good cook she needs someone who knows something about high-class entertaining. It's a rather exacting position, not everyone would be able to manage it. Do you think you could?'

Surprisingly, Paula felt a stir of interest. If she knew anything about anything, it was entertaining. Her parents had given so many dinner parties she thought she could do one in her sleep! It wryly amused her that a working knowledge of such functions, which she had so often considered a waste of time, should come in useful. She felt drawn towards the Americans because Luke's grandmother had been an American. He'd had a faint inflection of it in his voice. The Martins might remind her of him, but for that very reason she couldn't resist agreeing to work for them. 'I think I could manage very well,' she said.

As the Martins required someone urgently, she agreed to start straight away. They had a house near Hyde Park, which was quite a distance from where she lived and meant an early start, but Paula didn't mind. Jeff Martin wasn't in, but his wife was. A maid showed Paula into the lounge where Alexa Martin was waiting for her. Paula sensed that she was impatient as she kept glancing at her watch.

She stared at Paula intently as she walked towards her. 'You're my new cook-housekeeper? I can't quite believe it!' she exclaimed.

# CHAPTER TEN

PAULA decided it might be wiser to ignore her new employer's incredulity, which might only have to do with her youth. She had probably been expecting a middle-aged woman, rather than a girl of twenty-two.

'The agency sent me, Mrs Martin,' she replied, with a nervousness she hoped didn't show. 'I'm Paula Edison.'

'Oh, good!' Mrs Martin, recovering her poise, smiled brightly and shook Paula's hand. 'I'm not usually like a cat on hot bricks, dear, but I help my husband, and I'm late.'

'I'll be here earlier in the morning,' Paula assured her, 'now I know the way.'

Mrs Martin immediately looked dismayed. 'I was hoping, whoever the bureau sent, they'd be able to live in. We must discuss that this evening.'

There was a lot Paula would have liked to discuss now, but she could see that any questions would have to wait. 'I won't keep you,' she said. 'If you can give me some idea of what you'd like me to do today, while you're out, I'm sure I'll be able to manage.'

'Well, thank goodness you don't panic!' Mrs Martin, a beautiful brown-haired woman of about forty, breathed an audible sigh of relief at Paula's apparent coolness. 'I have six people coming for dinner. My husband and I do a lot of entertaining, and I'll have to leave the menu to you. I just haven't had time to get anything worked out.'

Paula didn't see this as an insurmountable problem and said so. Getting the quantities right, not the content, would be the difficult part. 'Please don't worry,' she remembered to add, 'madam. I'll take care of everything.'

'You're sure?' Mrs Martin frowned.

'Yes.' Paula almost believed in her own confidence. 'You can leave everything to me. There's only one or two things that it's perhaps important that I should know. Is there anything you wouldn't want me to serve? One of your guests could be allergic to something? And will the maid who showed me in be able to tell me where everything is?'

'That was Helen Barnes,' Mrs Martin hurriedly explained. 'She certainly knows where everything is as she's been with me for weeks. She's really a treasure, because she doesn't mind about long hours. You won't upset her, will you?'

'Of course not,' Paula smiled.

Mrs Martin talked quickly. She left the same way, in a flurry of half-finished sentences and last-minute instructions as she hurried out to a waiting taxi, leaving Paula dazed but not too alarmed.

Paula had approached her new job apprehensively, still suspicious of the change in herself. She had feared she might wake late that morning, as she had used to, and dismiss her agreement to cook for someone as temporary insanity and return to discontent and modelling. She had woken at six, wondering if Luke would be waiting for his breakfast, but not even the stark realisation that she wasn't still on Sabina had made her change her mind about going to work for the Martins. She was glad she hadn't when she realised that the hard work involved in such a demanding position might be enough to stop her from thinking continually of Luke Armstrong.

If there was to be a new interest in her life, it had to be involved with work. During the week since leaving Luke, she hadn't paused long enough to think of him properly. The nights were the most difficult, but she had a few sleeping tablets left over from when her parents died, when everything had suddenly got too much for her, and, after her first sleepless night, when she nearly made herself ill sobbing for him, she had taken one ever since, and at least they ensured she got a good night's sleep.

Unfortunately they left her feeling fuzzy-headed the next morning, which wouldn't do if she was to make a success of her new job. She hoped the novelty of different surroundings and the necessary concentration that cooking for Mrs Martin would entail would tire her enough to enable her to sleep naturally. The leaden weight in her heart, which was the certain knowledge that she wouldn't see Luke again, wasn't something that would go away, but if she persevered some of the agony might fade. The first morning after she returned from the Caribbean, she had been passing a bookshop. It had beckoned her like a laser beam; she had gone inside and found his books. His latest hardback she hadn't read, and she had almost emptied her purse trying to pay for it.

The assistant, glancing at her curiously, had alerted her to the fact that she was on the verge of breaking down, and when she had returned home she had tried to reason with herself. First love, a first affair, had to be traumatic. Feelings she had never imagined herself capable of had been born and developed, known perfect completion, then the shock of rejection. It had started a kind of madness, but if she tried hard enough, refused to pander to a crying need for one man, it might stop short of becoming an addiction. It must, she thought desperately, for without Luke there was no way she could satisfy the craving inside herself.

Instead of remembering how tender he could be, she concentrated on how he had been the last time she had seen him—the cold, implacable expression on his face, the hardness of his mouth and grey eyes. The intense dislike in them as he had said goodbye to her was as good an antidote as any when longing for him drove her to despair. He would be in New York now, forgetting her, with help from Monica and probably other beautiful girls.

The maid, Helen, was hardworking and inclined to be talkative. Paula soon learned everything there was to know about the general layout of the house. There were six bedrooms, a large dining-room, lounges and the usual domestic offices. The kitchen was a dream; Paula only hoped her cooking lived up to it!

She didn't ask Helen any personal questions about the family, but sometimes she chattered about them, and without seeming rude it would have been impossible to shut her up. Paula was told that the Martins were in London opening another branch of one of their international firms.

'Mrs Martin's a real lady,' Helen said admiringly, 'And I've heard people say she's a genius when it comes to business, which makes it seem strange that she's apt to panic in the kitchen. Yet when her last cook had to be rushed to hospital for an emergency, Madam took care of everything.'

'Had your last cook been here long?' asked Paula.

'Just a month,'

Helen reminded her of a sparrow of indefinable age as she sent her a bird-like glance. 'How did a girl like you happen to go after a job like this? A victim of circumstances, are you?'

Paula smiled slightly. Helen was very near the truth, although she suspected she was referring to the current unemployment. 'Not really,' she replied evasively. 'I didn't go to university and I had to do something and this kind of work seems more available than anything else at the moment.'

'I could swear I've seen your face somewhere before.' Helen stared at her. 'I'm not one to forget, but . . .'

'I think we should concentrate on Mrs Martin's dinner party,' Paula said quickly, though with a smile so Helen wouldn't take offence. 'I'd like to make a good impression my first day here. By the way, Mrs Martin said nothing about lunch. Do they come home for it?'

'No, dear,' Helen informed her. 'They usually have it out, except sometimes at weekends, so you don't have that to worry about.'

Paula prepared a dinner of several courses which

delighted the Martins and impressed their guests. She hadn't been sure she could do it, but she hid her sense of relief. As the number of guests was small, Helen served the meal herself with some help from Mrs Martin. When they gave a really big dinner party, Helen told Paula, they usually hired another maid and a butler.

Paula was kept busy in the kitchen and after the last guest had gone, she was just putting on her coat to leave herself when Alexa Martin came in followed by her husband, a big man with something of Luke's decisiveness. They both congratulated her on her cooking, and on learning where she was going, insisted on ringing for a taxi to take her home.

'I really would like you to live in, dear,' Alexa repeated what she had said that morning.

'I suppose I could,' Paula conceded doubtfully. 'I do have a room, though . . .'

'Then close it up, or rent it out while you work for me,' smiled Alexa. 'Your salary remains the same whatever you do, so you may as well take advantage of it. It would be so much more convenient, my dear.'

So Paula found herself living with the Martins, in a large attic room, furnished as a bedsitter with its own small bathroom. Funnily enough, she took to it the moment she saw it. A month of living in such a place would be no hardship.

From the top of the house, she had a good view over London and often at night stood looking at the star-strewn skies when she couldn't sleep. She would think of the years she had wasted, which she might have used more constructively, and sigh. She had used modelling as a stopgap, a means of making money. She had gone to the Caribbean for the same reason, to trick Luke out of his island. It must be rough justice that in trying to cheat Luke, she had cheated herself out of any love he might have had for her. Yet, despite this, she knew she had reason to be grateful to him. Falling in love with him had somehow served to rip the scales from her eyes, revealing her as quite a different person from the one she had believed herself to be. Which would have been a good thing, she would tell herself bleakly, if only his ghost had been as easy to erase!

Mrs Martin came to the kitchen to have a word with her, one morning when she had been there two weeks. Helen was busy upstairs.

'Ah, Paula,' she smiled ruefully, 'I thought I should warn you there'll be twelve people coming for dinner tomorrow. I'll arrange for the extra help and Jeff will choose the wine, but you'll have to let him know what you're planning.'

'I'll do that,' Paula promised, then asked, 'Roughly what age group will your guests be in?' The Martins, she had discovered, had friends and business acquaintances of all ages, but one evening, when the guests were mostly younger, Mrs Martin thought they hadn't altogether appreciated the rather conservative fare Paula had dished up. Now, if she didn't say, Paula remembered to ask.

'Mixed, I'm afraid,' Mrs Martin frowned. 'And do call me Alexa, Paula.'

Paula liked her warm-hearted employer and couldn't help smiling. 'I can't imagine what people would think if they heard your cook addressing you by your first name!'

'I've never concerned myself over things like that,' Alexa said dismissively. 'You're a charming girl and I like you. I only wish I knew what you're doing in my kitchen instead of in one of your own.'

When Paula, caught off guard, frowned, Alexa pursued gently, 'Yes, I mean why aren't you married? I'd have thought some man would have snapped you up long ago, or are they all blind?'

'Perhaps.' Paula went suddenly pale.

Alexa's gaze sharpened. 'There is a man, somewhere?'

'Was,' Paula corrected dully.

'Oh, I am sorry—I shouldn't have pried. You poor thing!' Alexa exclaimed remorsefully. 'Would you like to talk about it?'

While Paula wasn't sure she appreciated the way Alexa expressed her sympathy, she couldn't doubt the genuine kindness and concern in the other woman's eyes. All the same, she was relieved when Jeff Martin put his head around the door and asked his wife if she intended coming to work that day. Alexa fled with a resigned sigh, leaving Paula thoroughly shaken and hoping that by the time she returned her employer would have forgotten their conversation.

A large dinner party wasn't the only thing Paula was called on to cope with the following day. Alexa rang from her office to tell her there would be one extra for dinner, her husband's cousin, and he was coming to stay.

'I'm not sure how long he'll be staying, Paula, but could you get Helen to make up a bed in the blue room? I think that one will be best. I could have done without this,' she complained.

When she got home that evening, Alexa hastened, with her usual exuberance to the kitchen, as if feeling compelled to explain. 'I don't mind having Jeff's cousin visiting, you know, dear. We're both very fond of him. It's just when he's with us the phone never stops ringing. He's so good-looking that there's always some woman desperate to get in touch with him. The snag is, he frequently leaves me to get rid of them and I have to spend hours listening to their sorry tales.'

Paula was glad she hadn't burdened Alexa with any of her own. 'His room is ready, anyway,' she soothed. 'Helen saw to it and I checked. And dinner's all under control.'

'Oh, good!' This appeared to cheer Alexa up, and Helen said cunningly that if Mrs Martin was going upstairs to get ready now, she would have time to come with her and run her bath.

The extra maid and butler arrived, the butler immediately taking charge of the dining-room, much to Paula's relief. The fruit juices and appetisers were already in and she was thinking of reheating the soup, when Helen whispered that she had just shown the house-guest to his room and could Paula hold everything back for a few minutes.

Blessing such inconsideration, Paula assured her, 'I'll try.' Why couldn't he have got here an hour ago, when he'd been expected? She didn't think any credit was due to him that nothing was spoiled and the food was as good, when served, as if the ten-minute delay had never happened.

It was late before the last guests and Helen and the temporary staff had gone. Paula decided it was time she went to bed if she was to be recovered enough from what had proved a rather exhausting evening to get breakfast the next morning. The last thing the butler had done before he left was to take coffee and sandwiches into the lounge for the Martins and their one remaining guest, so she knew they would need nothing more that night.

She went quietly upstairs, the murmur of voices she had heard on passing the lounge door fading as she climbed higher. She wasn't sure what she was thinking about when it happened, the feeling of being speared in the back by something that made her legs go suddenly weak. She was just about to start on the flight of steps leading up to the attic when a surge of indescribable feeling shot through her, swinging her around like a puppet with its force to meet Luke Armstrong's incredulous gaze.

For endless moments, as she gasped, he seemed to hover in front of her. It couldn't be true! she thought, fearing she was going to faint. She was swimming in the darkness of his eyes and horrified, as he drew nearer, to see the burning expression in them.

'What the hell are you doing here?' he asked roughly. 'You weren't among the guests.'

'I'm not a guest.' She wondered how she could sound so cool when her whole body was screaming with pain. If Luke wished to know what she was doing here, she wanted to ask him the same question. 'I work here,' she breathed.

'You're not seriously asking me to believe that?' he jeered tersely.

His eyes glittered savagely, she had to concentrate every bit of willpower she could find before she could continue answering coolly.

'I'm Mrs Martin's new cook. Whether you believe it or not is up to you.'

'You're damn right it is,' he retorted. 'I've never heard of anything so ridiculous! Knowing you, nothing could be that simple.'

'You told me often enough I should make something useful of my life,' she replied bitterly. 'If you don't believe I'm speaking the truth, you can always check. Of course, that surely depends on how well you know the Martins. They may consider it none of your business?'

'Jeff Martin's my cousin,' he returned tightly. 'I'm staying here.'

Why hadn't she guessed? If she hadn't been so shocked at seeing him, she might have done. She recalled once noting something in Jeff Martin that had reminded her of Luke—a certain decisive self-confidence. 'What are you going to do?' she quivered anxiously.

He spoke softly, his eyes never leaving her pale, distraught face. 'As you say, it would be pointless for you to lie when I only have to drag you downstairs and confront Alexa and Jeff. But your explanation had better be good!'

As his cutting glance lanced through her, Paula's heart felt as though every bit of blood was draining from it. She returned his stare with a hungry apprehension she wasn't aware of. He was exactly the same—but then he would be, wouldn't he, after just three weeks. His face might be a shade thinner, his mouth harder, but the flight across the Atlantic would be responsible for the grey tinge to his skin. Otherwise, he was the same Luke she continually hungered for. He kept her awake at nights longing for him, reliving how it had felt to be in his arms. An intolerable anguish gripped her. She loved him, but he was standing in front of her like a stranger. He might not have forgotten her, but there was no pleasure for him in seeing her again.

'I've just explained,' she faltered. 'You told me to do something useful and I'm doing it. I was tired of modelling, so I went to another agency and got this job.'

'My God!' he breathed. 'There has to be more to it than that. I remember why you came to Barbados. My cousin is a wealthy man. What are you trying to do to him—or get out of him, I wonder?'

Horrified, Paula whispered, 'You must be mad!'

He ignored this. 'Have you told Jeff about your little escapade in Barbados? Or furnished any references?'

'My solicitor gave me one.'

'Did you tell Jeff?' Luke persisted ruthlessly.

'No!' she cried wildly, suddenly flying from him in panic up the steps to her attic and slamming the door. The door might have crashed in his face if he hadn't been too quick for her. Stopping it with a swiftly inserted foot, he closed it behind him derisively as he followed her into the room. Then he turned the key in the lock and put it in his pocket. 'To make sure we aren't interrupted,' he snapped meaningly.

As she recalled how Monica had burst in on them in his study on Sabina, Paula's dilated eyes glazed. 'I—I had no idea you had anything to do with the Martins,' she gasped, 'or I would never have been here.'

'And I had no idea you'd cooked the delectable dinner I ate.'

'Is—Monica with you?'

'No, damn you, she's not.'

'I only asked,' she mumbled weakly. Why did he sound as if he considered it her fault? 'Some other woman . . .?'

'Again, no,' he bit out. 'I've taken two to bed,' he told her cruelly, 'since I've been in New York, but not Monica.'

Paula felt incredibly hurt, her green eyes became drenched with tears. 'I realise your opinion of me, Luke, but I promise you I don't know the first thing about your cousin's affairs. And I'm only here for two more weeks. If you really do believe I have criminal intentions then you must tell him. I know I did wrong on Barbados, but I've paid for it since and done everything I could to put things right. I can't go around talking about it. I don't think it would serve any useful purpose, a lot of people would merely regard it as a joke, but you have a perfect right to protect your cousin and his wife from me, if you think it necessary.'

Luke said thickly, his eyes smouldering, 'You're so damned beautiful it gets in the way of clear thinking. It makes it impossible to tell how sincere you are. I may be a fool for giving you the benefit of the doubt, but that's all you're getting. I'll be right behind you, watching you, though, until your time here is up. One false move and I'll denounce you without compunction.'

'I'll leave.'

'No, you won't!' he muttered between his teeth. 'I have no evidence but my own suspicions that you're up to something again, and I've no wish to antagonise my favourite relatives by depriving them of their cook.'

'Why must you stay here?' she sighed, turning away from the anger in his eyes.

'It's convenient.'

'Well, you shouldn't be in my bedroom,' she said quickly, 'Alexa wouldn't like it.'

'Alexa, is it?'

Thick lashes lifted defiantly. 'She asked me to call her that. I don't always, but because she's so friendly it doesn't mean she'd approve of your being here. In fact I'm sure she wouldn't!'

A muscle Paula remembered twitched in the side of his jaw. 'She'd better get used to it,' he replied uncompromisingly, his eyes lifting from her anxious face to glance around the room. 'A very cosy set-up.

I'm sure I'll find it relaxing to spend an occasional evening here. I'm not that keen on the constant round of entertainment that Alexa and Jeff appear to consider necessary for their survival.'

Helplessly Paula gazed at him, trembling at even the thought of him perhaps stretched out on her bed. 'I'd like to be friendly, Luke, but not that friendly. You'd better stay downstairs.'

'Friends?' His eyes returned to her icily. 'Lady, do you know what you're asking?' Suddenly his arms shot out to pull her close to him, taking her by surprise. One of his hands slid to the bottom of her spine, the other to the nape of her neck, and his head blocked out the light.

Her first mistake was to fight him; she wanted to fight him, rather than be humiliated by her own starved response. Luke never liked being thwarted and he used his greater strength to subdue her struggles. His mouth was crueller than it might have been if she had immediately clung to him, as he crushed her lips against her teeth. The hand that shaped her neck was hot and she could feel the heat of his skin burning her through his shirt as he forced her lips apart. Then she sank against him in shock, completely stunned by the force of emotion shaking her. She went up like dry tinder, opening her mouth under his, becoming conscious of nothing but the feel and touch of him, of what his urgent masculinity was doing to her starved senses.

He whispered something, his mouth scorching her face while his hand on her hips pulling her close to him proved he was as aroused as she was. But even as her body melted and trembled, became overwhelmed by a driving, aching need, he was pushing her away, the very force of his movements savagely denying the sudden upsurge of devastating feeling between them.

Slowly she opened her eyes as she heard the door slam and realised he was gone. She was shaken as if she had been hurtling to the stars, then flung abruptly down to earth again. Luke hated her, his bitter resentment lay like a chasm between them. She had felt the depth of his desire and his repudiation of it. Her body burned and her mouth still throbbed from his kisses, but the apparent ease with which he had discarded her soon chilled the blood in her veins. Gulping back sobs, she sank down on her bed and hid her suddenly cold face in her hands.

Why was Luke here? He had said he was staying in New York. What had brought him to London? Obviously it had to be business, and he might not be staying long, but how could she live in the same house with him? She didn't doubt his ability to make her life miserable if he wanted to. What would she do, for instance, when he began taking other women out? Hadn't Alexa hinted that they were always chasing him, and hadn't he, by his own admission, revealed how much he needed a woman, if only to go to bed with? How was she to hide her hurt and unhappiness, even if it was only for another two weeks? Luke's arrival had been a shock, and even if his visit was shorter than he hinted, would she have sufficient willpower and pride to see her through it?

She rose at her usual time, next morning, and was startled to find Luke in the kitchen. He was wearing a pair of jeans and a dark sweater, and something happened to her breath as she stared at him.

'Doesn't this bring back memories of old times?' he gibed, raising his coffee cup in mocking salute as he took in her obvious dismay.

'Hardly old times,' she retorted, grabbing the hot percolator like a lifebelt. 'It's just been three weeks.'

Beneath his black brows, his eyes glittered with sudden anger which was reflected in the hand that grasped her thin arm. 'Time has passed quickly since you left me, has it?'

His eyes stared at her so hotly she felt scorched. Didn't he realise every day for her had stretched like a life sentence? 'It hasn't passed quickly,' she whispered, unable to control a compulsion to be honest with him.

Hadn't she vowed never again to conceal the truth from him? It might be hard, but no other course was open to her. If he asked she would even tell him how much she still loved him, but she hoped he wouldn't.

A flicker of doubt tightened his mouth, but he let go of her so she could drink her coffee. 'Why up so early?' he asked abruptly.

'I must have got into the habit on Sabina,' she answered as briefly. 'I don't seem able to sleep late now. Usually I go for a walk.'

'Jogging?' he asked.

'Not yet,' she smiled nervously. 'I'm thinking about it.'

'You'd look good in a leotard,' he said broodingly, his eyes wandering over her intimately, as though his remark gave him an excuse. As the colour crept hotly into Paula's cheeks as his eyes lingered on her breasts, he added softly, 'If you're going anywhere this morning, I'll come with you.'

They left the house together, Paula unable to resist his company. When they returned an hour later, her cheeks were glowing and there was an unconscious radiance in her eyes. As they went upstairs, they bumped into Alexa coming from her room. She looked surprised when she saw them together and her brows rose slightly at the proprietorial way in which Luke was holding Paula's arm, but there was humour in her faint smile rather than disapproval.

'So you've got to know each other?'

'Paula worked for me on Sabina,' Luke shook Paula by remarking coolly. 'It's more a case of renewing our acquaintance.'

'Oh, I see. What a coincidence!' exclaimed Alexa, glancing wide-eyed from Luke to Paula and back again. 'Did you know Paula was here?'

'No,' he grinned, 'you could have knocked me down with a feather. She didn't know I'd be here, either.'

'Well,' said Alexa, with her first hint of disapproval, 'I hope you won't try and inveigle her away. I thought of trying to entice her back to the States with me.'

'You can forget about that,' he made Paula gasp by replying calmly. 'I have other plans for her.'

Paula, on the brink of protesting, read the warning in his eyes in time. He had no plans, as such, for her; he was merely protecting his cousin. After the next two weeks, he wanted her as far away from his family as possible.

'I must have a wash and get breakfast started,' she said flatly, freeing herself from Luke. 'I'll see you later, Mrs Martin.'

Alexa came to the kitchen before she left for the office. She looked as though she was bursting to have a heart-to-heart talk, but thought better of it.

'There won't be anyone for lunch, dear. Luke is meeting an old—er—friend and we're all going out for dinner. I'm sure you must be tired after last night, so why don't you take the rest of the day off? Helen will be here if anyone wants anything.'

Why not? Paula asked herself, hiding despair. Luke was meeting another woman; Alexa had almost bitten her tongue off trying to conceal it. Was she that transparent? she wondered bitterly, doing her best to endure Alexa's pitying glance.

'My flat could do with a good going over,' she made an effort to laugh. 'I might even spend the night there, if you're sure you won't need me?'

'I'm sure,' Alexa said soothingly.

As Paula made her way across London, she felt grateful that Alexa hadn't warned her against Luke. At least she had been spared that! Her flat wasn't nearly in such need of attention as she'd pretended it to be. She had given that excuse on impulse, in order to avoid Luke, but the pain that was eating her up wouldn't let her rest. He wouldn't know where she was, he couldn't pursue her here with his taunts until she was begging for mercy. This morning he had acted strangely. Suddenly, for no apparent reason, he had begun being charming to her, slanting her little secret glances that made her pulse rate increase as if she had been running.

They had walked swiftly, but she could have been crawling along the ground, or standing still, she had become so lost in a kind of ecstasy. The knowledge that he was lunching with another woman had drained all sense of happiness from her.

After finishing a lot of unnecessary jobs, she decided to have a shower. She had switched on the heater when she first came in, so the water was hot. When she had finished she wrapped herself in a huge towel while she dried her hair. Then, to her dismay, there was a knock on the door.

It was after eight. Before reaching her room, she had done a little shopping and had some coffee in a snack bar, so it had been late afternoon before she had made a start on the housework. She didn't know any of her neighbours and no one knew she was here; it must be someone canvassing for something, or perhaps making enquiries about the last tenant.

Opening the door a cautious inch, she swayed with shock when her eyes encountered Luke's. Before she could speak or even try to shut him out, he had forced his way past her and banged the door.

'Do you always push your way in?' she gasped, backing from him helplessly.

He caught her easily, holding her roughly, taking no notice when the towel fell from her head as she took a firmer grip of the one round her shaking body. 'When you've searched the entire town for eight hours,' he rasped, 'you don't feel like being polite.'

'For—me?' she whispered hoarsely.

'Yes, you!' his teeth snapped. 'You weren't at the address I wrung out of the Cranfords. The couple living there now are away on their honeymoon. A neighbour said you'd moved but she didn't know where. I was going crazy when Jeff remembered the address you'd given to the taxi driver who'd taken you home the first night you worked for them.'

'You're dressed?' she queried somewhat incoherently as her eyes wandered dazedly over the black evening suit which so enhanced his magnificient figure.

'Of course I'm dressed,' he glared. 'Jeff couldn't remember at first. It was only by constant prodding on my part that he did—halfway through dinner at the Savoy.'

'You—walked out?'

'I should think they were glad to see the back of me,' he admitted with a twisted grin. 'Alexa said she understood my dilemma, but my constant badgering of Jeff was spoiling her evening.'

'Why did you want to see me so urgently?' Paula asked stiffly. 'You surely can't believe it's necessary to keep an eye on me to this extent?'

'That has nothing to do with it,' he said curtly.

'You say you've been looking for me all day,' she whispered, her throat so achingly tight it was painful to talk. 'Yet Alexa distinctly told me you were taking some woman out to lunch.'

'That woman was you!' he snapped impatiently. 'I admit I didn't mention you by name. I feared, if I did, she might believe you needed protecting and find you something to do. I thought I mightn't stand a chance against the combined resistance of the two of you. Then I got held up on the phone and when I came to find you, you'd gone. I've been searching for you ever since.'

'I can't think why,' she replied, and, as her towel slipped, reminding her of how little she had on, 'but if you've anything more to tell me, you'll have to wait outside until I get dressed.'

His eyes swerved to the wide bed, the two armchairs which clearly indicated that she had just one room. 'I'm not leaving,' he said. 'You may have a fire escape and I'm taking no chances. I'll turn my back, but that's all.'

Paula didn't want to make an issue of it. The only way she might get through the next few minutes was to keep a cool head. With a shrug, she found an old caftan in her closet and squeezed herself into the small cubicle that was her bathroom to get rid of the towel and put it on. As calmly as possible, when she returned, she picked up a brush and attempted to restore a little order to her tangled curls.

Luke closed the gap between them, like a man nearing the limit of human endurance. 'Leave it,' he ordered thickly, taking the brush from her. 'You're beautiful however you are, whatever you're doing.' Suddenly his arms were around her, lifting her to the bed. Sitting on the edge of it, he held her tightly, pressing his cheek against hers. 'I can't do without you, Paula. I finally realised it in the park this morning. Let me stay, don't send me away again.'

Paula's fragile control broke with a snap as she was crushed to the hardness of his chest. 'I didn't before!' she breathed, unable to understand him.

'You said you loved me, but I couldn't believe you,' he muttered raggedly. 'I thought you were just using it as an excuse for letting me make love to you. Women are apt to say—I would never have let you near me if I hadn't cared. They find excuses, as men do, for enjoying sex.'

'You had sex in New York,' her trembling voice reproached him. 'With two women.'

'Darling,' he confessed gruffly, 'I lied about that. I was desperate to reassure myself I could get over you if I tried, but I never got further than kissing them on their respective doorsteps. I realised, even before I got as far as that, that it was no good.'

'And Monica?' she breathed, trembling as his hands constantly tightened on her thinly clad body.

'She was only a smoke-screen,' he grimaced, his lips against her ear. 'It was a complete surprise when she and her friends turned up on Sabina, but because I was desperate I let them stay. She did have a small part in one of my films and she's hoping to be in my next play, but otherwise there's never been anything between us. On Sabina I never touched her.'

Paula whispered rawly, 'I saw you carry her into her bedroom one evening.'

Luke drew a sharp breath. 'I didn't mean you to see that. She was drunk. She actually fell twice and I could see her breaking her neck on the stairs, though by that time I might have welcomed it. I stayed with her while she was sick, then dumped her in bed, that was all.'

Paula believed him. She also wanted to believe the urgent kisses he was pressing on her neck and throat. They were like the kisses of a man who wanted her. It took a lot of willpower to ease slightly away from him.

'I still don't know why you're here?'

'Because I had to find you!' he breathed. 'I endured New York as long as I could and came to beg you to overlook the past and begin again. I tried to give you more time to decide exactly how you felt about me, but all I could see was the misery in your eyes as we said goodbye on Barbados. All I craved for was to find you and hold you, to wipe away your tears.'

'But the past was my doing,' she whispered unhappily.

'When I thought about it,' he replied dryly, 'I realised how unimportant it was. I also realised the total sum of your experience. I talked to Denis Cranford today, when I went there to see if he could help me to find you. After telling me you'd left your luxury flat, he told me a few more things. He said you hadn't been keen to work for him and he didn't think you'd realised what you were taking on. He also said you'd refused any kind of reimbursement.'

'If I didn't realise what I was taking on,' Paula interrupted, feeling compelled to be honest, 'it was probably because I was concentrating more on the rewards than what was involved. I was having to improvise as I went along, and frequently panicked. But while I often regretted what I was doing, it wasn't until I was living on your island that I knew real remorse.'

Luke's lips found hers grimly. 'I think I could have killed you when I discovered what you were up to,' he muttered. 'I was falling in love with you, and I'd never been in love before. The sheer rage and disillusionment that brought on convinced me I didn't care for you any more, but I knew I was fooling myself when I made love to you.'

'Was that why you kept me on Sabina?'

'Not exactly,' he confessed. 'Until then I'd believed you were experienced. I was sure you couldn't have been engaged to Ian Doobray and not been. I was forced to do a lot of rethinking.'

'Until then I thought—I'd thought I was frigid.'

'Frigid?' A surge of dark red colour crept under his skin. 'Darling!' he groaned, turning her face so he could cover it again with urgent kisses as his other hand possessively curved her breast. 'I'd never known anything as warm and exciting as you were that night. That was partly why I didn't let you go. I couldn't believe that such a coming together could be free of consequences. I had to keep you there until I was sure. I couldn't bear the thought of you leaving and either getting rid of my son or daughter, or having to face bearing my child alone. When I made love to you the second night, after vowing never to touch you again, I really went out of my mind. Monica's arrival, the next morning seemed like the answer to a desperate cry for help. Having her watching my every move took a lot of putting up with, but it helped me to keep my hands off you. Some of the time!' he ended dryly.

'Oh, Luke darling!' Paula blinked back the tears that had accumulated as she listened to him. Looking into his smouldering eyes, she slid her arms around his neck. 'Sabina was a revelation to me, in more ways than one. When my parents died I was furious with them for leaving me no money. I got engaged to Ian, not because I loved him but for the title that will one day be his, and I was even more resentful when he threw me over. I went to Barbados because I was too lazy to earn enough to pay my rent, and somehow believing that in fooling you I would be avenging myself of Ian, and I hadn't even the guts to see the job I'd agreed to do for the Cranfords through. But even when you exposed me, I was far from being repentant. It wasn't until I became aware that I loved you, and you'd made love to me, that I knew how much I'd changed. I scarcely recognised myself after that. I lost interest in all the flimsy, transient things I'd thought so important. I wanted to make something of my life, if I couldn't be your wife.'

For the first time a hint of humour broke the tautness of Luke's face. 'You wouldn't by any chance be proposing to me?'

'Oh . . .' she refused to look coy, but colour stung her high cheekbones as she became aware of what she had said. 'I'm sorry, Luke.'

'Don't be,' he begged huskily. 'Ever since our bogus engagement ended I've been kicking myself for not making it real. I was furious afterwards for not letting you continue believing you'd fooled me until I'd trapped you into marrying me. I thought I'd got the better of you, but I'd really outsmarted myself.'

'I wish you'd made me marry you then, Luke,' she whispered, pressing tiny fevered kisses on his cheek. 'I learned to love Sabina.'

'We'll return there for our honeymoon,' he kissed her softly back. 'I want to wake up in the morning and see the sunrise with you in my arms. I want to make love to you until you forget everything but me.'

'I've thought of nothing but you for a long time,' she confessed.

'I got the shock of my life when I found you working for my cousin and his wife.' His hands were busy with her zip.

'I intended training to be a nannie, after that.'

'A nannie?' He concentrated on easing the caftan over her creamy shoulders. 'Well, it's a thought,' he teased. 'But if you feel like taking care of any children, I think they'd better be mine.'

'Oh, Luke,' she exclaimed helplessly, 'I love you so much, it will be a pleasure.'

'And I you,' he murmured thickly, pressing her down on the bed.

They kissed, their mouths touching and tasting, their bodies moving in the slow, rapturous rhythm of love.

Then his arms came around her and he crushed her
against him with a groan. Sanity abandoned Paula as
suddenly Luke's restraint broke and they were caught in
the grip of a more powerful emotion than either had
experienced before. She responded to the hard pressure
of his hot mouth on hers with a passion that matched
his own. Their coming together released more than a
hint of savagery in both of them. As he rained a trail of
burning kisses from her lips to her throat, a sweet
aching torment that only he could quench rippled
through her. And Luke's deep and ragged breathing
told her he was no more immune to the inferno of
frenzied desire than she was.

She was so eager to belong to him completely that it
came as a shock when a shudder ran visibly through his
hard body and he suddenly pushed her away.

'I want you,' he groaned, pulling her against him
again, as he saw the anguished longing on her face,
'don't ever doubt it, my darling, but the next time I
make love to you has to be when we're married. You
have to believe that it's love, not just lust, I feel for you,
and somehow I know that waiting will cancel out the
past and make everything come all right.'

'But—Luke,' she objected, unable to think of
anything but how her body was burning for him.

'Hush!' he whispered thickly, his eyes devouring her
'You have to help me, Paula. It isn't easy for me either,
but we can be married and on Sabina in a few days.'

Gulping, she frowned, 'But Alexa?'

'I'll find her another cook, even if it kills me!' he
declared firmly. 'Alexa may not like it, but she'll
understand when I explain that my need is greater than
hers. I come from a large family, I have cousins all over
the world, but I'm only ever going to have one wife.'

Paula traced a finger over the sensual line of his
mouth. 'I must be completely without conscience, that I
can abandon my post so easily.'

He laughed, kissing her fingers, his eyes full of love
and trust. 'As long as you abandon yourself to me!

Now, I think we'd better get back to the house. I
believe I'm due for some congratulations.'

Dreamily she tried again to dissuade him. 'I don't
have to return tonight.'

White teeth glinting, he brought them both quickly to
their feet, giving her a playful smack that made her
nerves tingle. 'We have a wedding to plan, to say
nothing of a cook to replace. We haven't time to waste
here, woman!'

'Oh, Luke . . .!'

Catching her to him, he kissed her fiercely. 'You're
like fire in my blood. I love you, I won't ever let you
go.'

His face sobered, and Paula, seeing the darkening
need in his eyes, trembled as her heart began beating
faster again. It seemed incredible that Luke loved her
and she was going to be his wife. For the first time in
her life she knew utter contentment and a consuming
urge to put another's happiness before her own. Luke
would return every measure of happiness she gave him,
though. She knew she could count on that.

'I'll never ask you to let me go, my darling,' she
whispered, looking at him with glowing eyes. 'All I'll
ever need is you.'

# Coming Next Month in Harlequin Presents!

**863  MATCHING PAIR  Jayne Bauling**
A lounge singer and a hotel owner are two of a kind. He chooses to
live life on the surface; she feels she has no choice. Neither have
been touched by love.

**864  SONG OF A WREN  Emma Darcy**
Her friend and lodger, a terrible tease, introduces her to his family
in Sydney as his "live-in lady." No wonder his brother deliberately
downplays their immediate attraction.

**865  A MAN WORTH KNOWING  Alison Fraser**
A man worth knowing, indeed! An English secretary decides that
an American author is not worth getting involved with...as if the
choice is hers to make.

**866  DAUGHTER OF THE SEA  Emma Goldrick**
A woman found washed ashore on a French Polynesian island
feigns amnesia. Imagine her shock when her rescuer insists that
she's his wife, the mother of his little girl!

**867  ROSES, ALWAYS ROSES  Claudia Jameson**
Roses aren't welcome from the businessman a London *pâtisserie*
owner blames for her father's ruin. She rejects his company, but
most of all she rejects his assumption that her future belongs
with him.

**868  PERMISSION TO LOVE  Penny Jordan**
Just when a young woman resigns herself to a passionless
marriage to satisfy her father's will, the man in charge of her
fortune and her fate withholds his approval.

**869  PALE ORCHID  Anne Mather**
When a relative of his wrongs her sister, a secretary confronts the
Hawaiian millionaire who once played her for a fool. She expects
him to be obstructive—not determined to win her back.

**870  A STRANGER'S TOUCH  Sophie Weston**
One-night stands are not her style. Yet a young woman cannot
deny being deeply touched by the journalist who stops by her
English village to recover from one of his overseas assignments.

*Can you keep a secret?*

## You can keep this one plus 4 free novels